My dearest puppy, Storm,

I hope this letter reaches you safe and sound. You have been so brave since you had to flee from the evil wolf Shadow.

Do not worry about me. I will hide here until you are strong enough to return and lead our pack. For now you must move on – you must hide from Shadow and his spies. If Shadow finds this letter I believe he will try to destroy it . . .

Find a good friend – someone to help finish my message to you. Because what I have to say to you is important. What I have to say is this: you must always

Please don't feel lonely. Trust in your friends and all will be well.

Your loving mother,

Canista

Sue Bentley's books for children often include animals, fairies and wildlife. She lives in Northampton and enjoys reading, going to the cinema, relaxing by her garden pond and watching the birds feeding their babies on the lawn. At school she was always getting told off for daydreaming or staring out of the window – but she now realizes that she was storing up ideas for when she became a writer. She has met and owned many cats and dogs and each one has brought a special kind of magic to her life.

Sue Bentley

Magic Puppy

Star of the Show
& Party Dreams
& A Forest Charm

Illustrated by Angela Swan

PUFFIN

To Butch – a boisterous playmate with a mind of his own
To Molly – fun little Westie run-around
Charlie – cute funny-face, cat lover

PUFFIN BOOKS

Published by the Penguin Group
Penguin Books Ltd, 80 Strand, London WC2R ORL, England
Penguin Group (USA) Inc., 375 Hudson Street, New York, New York 10014, USA
Penguin Group (Canada), 90 Eglinton Avenue East, Suite 700, Toronto, Ontario, Canada M4P 2Y3
(a division of Pearson Penguin Canada Inc.)
Penguin Ireland, 25 St Stephen's Green, Dublin 2, Ireland (a division of Penguin Books Ltd)
Penguin Group (Australia), 250 Camberwell Road, Camberwell, Victoria 3124, Australia
(a division of Pearson Australia Group Pty Ltd)
Penguin Books India Pvt Ltd, 11 Community Centre, Panchsheel Park, New Delhi – 110 017, India
Penguin Group (NZ), 67 Apollo Drive, Rosedale, North Shore 0632, New Zealand
(a division of Pearson New Zealand Ltd)
Penguin Books (South Africa) (Pty) Ltd, 24 Sturdee Avenue, Rosebank, Johannesburg 2196, South Africa

Penguin Books Ltd, Registered Offices: 80 Strand, London WC2R ORL, England

puffinbooks.com

Magic Puppy: Star of the Show first published 2008
Magic Puppy: Party Dreams first published 2008
Magic Puppy: A Forest Charm first published 2008
First published in one volume 2010
001 – 10 9 8 7 6 5 4 3 2 1

Text copyright © Sue Bentley, 2008
Illustrations copyright © Angela Swan, 2008
All rights reserved

The moral right of the author and illustrator has been asserted

Set in Bembo 15/22 pt
Typeset by Palimpsest Book Production Limited, Falkirk, Stirlingshire
Made and printed in Great Britain by Clays Ltd, St Ives plc

British Library Cataloguing in Publication Data
A CIP catalogue record for this book is available from the British Library

ISBN: 978-0-141-33193-5

www.greenpenguin.co.uk

Magic Puppy

Star of the Show

Prologue

The young silver-grey wolf froze as a
terrifying howl rose into the air.

'Shadow!' Storm gasped. The big,
fierce lone wolf, who had attacked
Storm's pack and left his mother
wounded, was very close.

Suddenly a dazzling flash of bright
golden light and a shower of sparks
filled the air. Where the young wolf had

stood there now crouched a tiny rusty-coloured spaniel puppy with wavy fur, long floppy ears and midnight-blue eyes.

Storm's puppy heart beat fast as he bounded forward across the snow. He looked from left to right, trying to find a hiding place, but the flat plain stretched in all directions like a white desert.

He saw a tiny speck in the distance, which was growing bigger as it came closer. It was an adult wolf.

Storm whimpered with terror.

His wobbly legs collapsed beneath him and Storm felt himself sinking. Chunks of snow rained on to the little puppy as he sank down into an ice cave. He lay there trembling, hoping that his hiding place would protect him.

Moments later, Storm heard paws scrabbling above him as a large animal enlarged the entrance to the cave. This was it. Shadow had dug him out!

A wolf's head appeared, framed by the night sky. 'Are you hurt, my son?' growled a soft velvety voice.

'Mother!' Storm woofed in relief, wagging his little tail. 'I am fine now!'

Canista slid right in and crouched beside her disguised cub. She licked his muzzle in greeting. 'I am glad to see you again, but it is not yet safe for you to return. Shadow is very close. He wants to lead the Moon-claw pack, but they will not follow him while you live.'

Storm's midnight-blue eyes sparked

with fear and anger. 'Perhaps we should face him and fight him!'

Canista showed her sharp white teeth in a proud smile. 'Bravely said, Storm. But Shadow is too strong for you to face alone. And I am still too weak from his poisonous bite to help you. Use this disguise. Go to the other world and return when you are stronger.' She winced and her eyes clouded with pain.

Storm huffed out a warm glittering puppy breath. It shimmered around Canista's wounded leg in a golden mist and then sank into her grey fur. 'Thank you. The pain is fading,' she rumbled softly.

Suddenly, another fierce howl seemed to tear at the icy air.

4

'Shadow is coming! Save yourself. Go . . .' Canista urged.

Bright gold sparks ignited in the tiny puppy's wavy reddish-brown fur. Storm whined as he felt the power building within him. The golden light around him grew brighter. And brighter . . .

Chapter
ONE

Tessa Churchill's tummy lurched with excitement as she saw all the huge trucks and trailers in front of Harpford Manor. There were lights and equipment everywhere and lots of people pushing trolleys and racks of costumes.

'I still can't believe that I'm going to be in *Timepiece* with Donny Jenton. I'm so nervous,' Tessa said to her mum.

'That's not surprising. This is your
first part in a film,' Mrs Churchill said,
giving her a hug. 'Come on, let's go
and find Judith Raunds, the lady who'll
be looking after you.'

Tessa nodded as she and her mum
began walking towards the main house.

She was also looking forward to meeting the other two girls who had parts in the film – Tessa had been excited to hear that they were about the same age as her. It would be great to hang out with new friends while she was here.

A woman came out of a side door and greeted them both. 'Hello, Mrs Churchill, I'm Judith. And this must be Tessa. I'm delighted to meet you.' She had a light-brown pony tail and a pleasant round face and was wearing a blue T-shirt, jeans and trainers.

Mrs Churchill shook Judith's hand. 'Hello, Judith. It's nice to put a face to the voice. And thanks for being so understanding when I phoned to say we'd be late arriving,' she said.

Judith smiled. 'No problem. Hold-ups at airports are a fact of life these days.' She turned to Tessa. 'Let's go inside. Kelly and Fay arrived earlier. They're having supper. I'll introduce you.'

'OK.' Tessa smiled at Judith who seemed really nice. She felt herself starting to relax. She turned to her mum. 'I'll be fine now. You don't have to stay with me.'

'Sure? All right then, darling. I'll get going.' Mrs Churchill kissed her daughter on the cheek. 'See you next week. And don't forget to phone.'

'You bet! Give my love to Dad when you get back to the yacht. Bye!' Tessa said. She waited until her mum drove off and then followed Judith into the house.

They went through a maze of
corridors until they reached a very
grand room. It had panelling on the
walls and a high domed ceiling,
which was painted with clouds and
cherubs. Expensive-looking paintings of
rather stern people were hung all
around.

A self-service counter with hot and
cold food had been set up along one
wall and there were neat rows of tables
and chairs. The room buzzed with
voices and laughter.

'This is where you'll have all your
meals. Catering is 24/7, so you can
get a hot drink or food whenever you
want it,' Judith explained. She led Tessa
over to two girls who were sitting at a
table by themselves. 'These are your

young co-stars, Kelly Lucas and Fay
Hinson. Kelly, Fay, this is Tessa
Churchill.'

'Hi,' Tessa said, smiling.

Fay and Kelly smiled back.

'I'll leave you all to get to know
one another. I've got a few things to
do, so I'll pop back in a bit and see if
you need anything,' Judith said to
Tessa.

'OK, thanks,' Tessa said, smiling at the two girls as Judith moved away.

Kelly's friendly expression suddenly changed. 'So you're the kid with posh parents. I bet you loved keeping everyone waiting, so you could get all the attention when you *finally* arrived!' She looked about twelve years old, two years older than Tessa, and had a thin face and short dark hair.

Tessa felt herself going red. At her first drama school, she'd been bullied because of having rich parents, so now she kept quiet about it. Kelly must have listened to Judith on the phone to her mum and heard about the holiday on the family yacht, which

Tessa was cutting short to work on this film.

Tessa took a breath to calm her nerves before answering, 'Let's get something straight, Kelly. Acting is all that matters to me and I just want to do my best, the same as you. So leave my mum and dad out of it. OK?' she said.

Kelly looked surprised and even a tiny bit impressed. She seemed about to say something else and then she shrugged. 'Whatever,' she said, getting up and wandering over to the service counter.

Tessa looked at Fay, hoping that the other girl might be easier to get on with. 'Which stage school do you come from?' she asked her.

'Ashton School of Drama,' Fay murmured without looking up. She was stirring her plate of pasta around with a fork and seemed to be in a world of her own.

Tessa tried again. 'Have you seen Donny Jenton yet?'

'No. Someone said they'd seen his

little pug dog, Lady. So he's here. But there's masses of security around him. We'll probably only get to meet Donny when we're acting in a scene with him,' Fay said gloomily. She pushed her plate away and drooped forward to rest her chin on her elbows.

Tessa felt her spirits sinking. Fay definitely didn't seem any more bothered than Kelly about making friends with her.

A wave of loneliness rose in Tessa as she wished that she'd asked her mum to stay for a bit longer. But she squared her shoulders and resolved to make the best of it.

Tessa decided to go straight up to her room and start unpacking. She didn't feel much like eating and there didn't seem much point in sitting here with Fay and Kelly.

Tessa rose to her feet. 'How do I get to our room?' she asked Fay.

Fay looked up at last. She had freckled skin and hazel eyes and would have been pretty if her face hadn't been screwed into a frown. 'Um . . . through that door, up two lots of stairs and turn left. It's the third room you come to.'

'Thanks.' As Tessa went out, she passed Kelly who was on her way back to the table with a glass of Coke. 'Too good to sit and eat with us, are you, Princess?' the older girl mocked.

Tessa ignored her, but to her annoyance she felt a lump rising in her throat as she remembered what it was

like to be bullied. Well, she wasn't a
scared little kid any more. She was ten
years old and had been in heaps of TV
adverts and theatre plays and she was
determined not to cry.

Bolting up the stairs two at a time,
Tessa found their room easily. She saw
that her suitcase had been brought up

and left on the rug. She looked around.
The two beds on either side of the
window had been taken. The only one
left was in a gloomy alcove. There was
barely room for the bed, a small bedside
cabinet and a battered-looking
wardrobe.

'This just gets better!' Tessa grumbled,
picking up her case and dumping it on
her bed. She opened her case, grabbed a
bundle of clothes at random and
opened the wardrobe. The door swung
wide with a loud, rusty squeak and
Tessa was blinded by a dazzling bright
gold flash.

'Oh!' Tessa gasped, staggering back.
When she could see again, Tessa saw a
tiny puppy with wavy reddish-brown
fur, floppy ears and bright midnight-

blue eyes looking up at her from the bottom of the wardrobe.

'Can you help me, please?' it woofed.

Chapter
TWO

Tessa stared down at the tiny puppy in complete surprise, wondering where it had come from. The wardrobe door squeaking open had made it sound like the puppy had spoken! Tessa shook her head at the silly idea.

'What are you doing in there?' she crooned, bending over to look more closely at the puppy. 'Aren't you cute? You look like a little spaniel.'

'I have arrived here from far away.
I am Storm of the Moon-claw pack.
Who are you?' the puppy woofed.

Tessa's eyes widened in shock and the
pile of clothes slipped from her numb
fingers and crumpled to the floor. 'You
really c-can talk,' she gasped in
amazement.

The puppy nodded, looking up at her with large, intelligent blue eyes, as if waiting for her to reply to its question. Although it was only tiny, it didn't seem to be very afraid of her.

'I'm . . . um . . . Tessa Churchill. I'm an actress. I'm here to make a film.'

The puppy dipped its tiny head in a formal bow. 'I am honoured to meet you, Tessa. I must hide. Can you help me?' he said in a gruff little bark.

'Is someone after you?' Tessa asked. She still couldn't quite believe that this was happening, but her curiosity was beginning to get the better of her shock.

Storm's big dewy eyes sparked with anger and fear. 'Shadow, the evil lone

wolf is looking for me. He has killed
my father and three litter brothers and
wounded my mother. He wants to lead
the Moon-claw pack but the other
wolves are waiting until I am strong
enough to lead them.'

Tessa frowned. 'But how can you lead
a wolf pack? You're just a pu—'

'I will show you! Please stand back,'
Storm interrupted in a soft bark.

He leapt out of the wardrobe and
stood on the carpet. There was another
dazzling flash of bright gold light and
sparks sprayed out, floating down
around Tessa and crackling where they
landed.

'Oh!' she gasped as the tiny puppy
vanished and in its place there stood a
muscular young silver-grey wolf. Tessa

nervously eyed the wolf's large sharp teeth and powerful paws that seemed much too big for his body. 'Storm?'

'Yes, Tessa, it is me. Do not be afraid. I will not harm you,' Storm growled gently.

Before Tessa had time to get used to the majestic sight of Storm as a young wolf, there was a final bright burst of light and he reappeared in the room as a tiny puppy with wavy rusty-coloured fur and a swishy tail.

'That's an amazing disguise. No one would know that you're a wolf,' Tessa said, deeply impressed.

'Shadow will know if he finds me. I need to hide now,' Storm whined.

Tessa saw that he was starting to tremble all over. With his startling midnight-blue eyes, wet reddish-brown nose and little pointed face, Storm was the most adorable thing she had ever seen.

Her soft heart went out to the helpless little puppy who needed a friend as much as she did.

'I'll look after you. You can sleep here with me –' she began and then stopped as she realized that pets probably wouldn't be allowed. 'I could try and hide you, but I'm sharing this room with two other girls. Fay's all wrapped up in herself, so she might not notice. But I bet Kelly would love to snitch on me, just to get me into trouble!' she guessed.

Storm showed his little pointed teeth in a doggy grin. 'I would love to stay

here with you, Tessa. I will use my
magic so that only you will be able to
see and hear me.'

'You can make yourself invisible?
Cool! Then there's no problem. You can
stay in here and Kelly and Fay won't
know a thing.' Tessa bent down to pick
Storm up and stroke his soft little head.

'Thank you, Tessa!' Storm snuggled up
to her, wagging his little red-brown tail.

She was glad of her bed in the dim alcove now. It would be much easier to cuddle up with Storm and talk to him without attracting attention from her room-mates.

As Tessa put Storm down and then picked up her clothes to hang them away, the tiny puppy jumped on to her duvet. He gave a contented sigh and curled up for a nap.

Tessa smiled to herself in delight. This was better than any film and Kelly's and Fay's unfriendliness didn't matter any more. She wouldn't be lonely now that she had this amazing magic puppy for company.

Tessa woke early the following morning. She could feel a warm weight tucked

into the crook of her arm. Feeling her
stir, Storm sat up and stretched.

'Hello, Storm. Did you sleep OK?'
Tessa whispered so that the other girls
couldn't hear her.

'Very well. This is a good place,'
Storm woofed.

The bedroom door opened and Judith
popped her head in. 'Rise and shine,
everyone!' she said brightly. 'Come
down for breakfast as soon as you can,
please. School lessons start in an hour.'

'OK. I'll be right there!' Tessa said.

Judith flashed a smile at her before
going out and closing the door.

'It's a shame that our schools have to
set work for us. I can't wait until I'm
older and then I can act all day,' Tessa
whispered to Storm.

Kelly jumped up, got straight out of bed and went to the bathroom, but Fay sat up blinking and rubbing her eyes sleepily.

Tessa wasn't surprised. Fay had been writing something in a big green book for ages before she went to sleep. It was there on top of her bedside cabinet.

'Is that your scrapbook?' Tessa asked
Fay. She knew that most kids who went
to stage schools kept a book of cuttings
and photos from their performances.

'It's my diary and it's private,' Fay said,
slipping the book into a drawer and
slamming it shut.

'OK. I only asked,' Tessa murmured as
she threw back her duvet and quickly
got dressed.

Storm trotted invisibly at Tessa's heel
as she came downstairs to the dining
room. The delicious smells of eggs and
bacon and toast floated towards them.
Tessa asked for a big breakfast and then
slipped bits of bacon and egg under the
table for Storm when no one was
looking.

Lessons with Judith started promptly.

Storm curled up for a nap on Tessa's lap. When a tiny rumbling snore rose from him, it was all Tessa could do to stifle her giggles.

It was history today and Tessa worked steadily, but she was glad when lessons finished for the day. 'I wonder when the director will want us,' she commented to Storm as she, Fay and Kelly tidied away their workbooks.

'Duh! When he's ready,' Kelly scoffed. 'Or maybe you think you deserve special treatment, Princess?'

Tessa flushed. She must have spoken louder than she meant to and Kelly had heard and thought she was talking to herself. She realized that she was going to have to be a lot more careful about keeping Storm a secret.

'Stop calling me "Princess"! I don't like it!' she snapped at Kelly.

'OK, Your Royal Highness,' Kelly crowed.

Chapter
THREE

'Fay Hinson, Kelly Lucas, Tessa
Churchill to wardrobe and make-up,
please!' a woman with a clipboard called
out later that afternoon.

Judith Raunds showed them the way
and they all set off eagerly.

'Yay! This is it. We're going to get
our costumes and have our hair and
make-up done,' Tessa whispered to

Storm as he trotted beside her.

There was a big sign that read 'Wardrobe' on one of the rooms. Inside thousands of gorgeous dresses hung in neatly labelled rows and there were countless shelves and racks of hats, gloves and shoes, and wigs on stands. Assistants fetched armfuls of Victorian clothes, complete with underwear, petticoats and black boots for the three girls.

As Tessa was helped into her costume, she noticed that her name was sewn into every item, just like a real movie star. Once the girls were dressed they went to hair and make-up. A whole hour passed before Fay, Kelly and Tessa were finished. Tessa hardly recognized herself under the curly brown wig! She

did a twirl in front of Storm so that
her skirts swung out with a silken
rustle.

Storm tucked his little rust-coloured
tail between his legs and looked up at
her with anxious midnight-blue eyes.

'What's wrong? Don't you like it?'
Tessa whispered after quickly checking
everyone was busy.

'It is a very good disguise,' Storm
woofed. 'But who is the fierce enemy
you are hiding from?'

'I'm not hiding from anyone,' Tessa reassured him. 'I have to wear this for the film, the same as Kelly and Fay. We're all dressed up because we're supposed to be three Victorian children who find a magic watch. We have to act in three scenes. You'll get the idea when you see us on set.'

'Where is on set?' Storm barked.

'It's anywhere the day's filming is going to be. They set up lights and bits of scenery. And the floor's marked out so you know where to stand to say your lines.'

Storm frowned. 'It sounds very strange.'

Tessa smiled. 'I expect it does if you're not used to it. Acting is really like

having the most brilliant game of
pretend. It's just the best.'

'I like games too, especially with balls
and sticks,' Storm yapped, looking much
happier.

'I'll see what I can do about that
later,' Tessa promised.

A young man with another clipboard
appeared at the door and called for
them to follow him to the rose garden
at the back of the house.

Tessa let Judith, Kelly and Fay walk
on ahead, so that she could talk to
Storm without anyone noticing. At first
the tiny puppy kept treading on her
long swishing skirts and almost
tumbling over his own paws.

'You'll have to walk a bit further
away or you'll get swept off your feet,'

Tessa told him, trying not to laugh and hurt his feelings.

Storm finally got the idea and padded behind Tessa, keeping his distance.

The rose garden was surrounded by clipped hedges. There was a pretend stone arch and a wrought-iron seat made of painted wood. Thick cables trailed across the ground and there were huge bright lights and cameras all over the place.

Tessa noticed that Fay went and stood all by herself. She was threading her fingers and looking very pale and tense. For the first time Tessa wondered if Fay's seeming unfriendliness was really just a bad attack of nerves.

A tall young man dressed in an old-fashioned dark suit and a shirt with a stiff, high collar walked through the stone arch.

'Look! That's Donny Jenton!' Tessa said excitedly.

'Wow! He's *much* better looking in real life, isn't he?' Kelly gushed.

Tessa bit back a grin. Kelly was obviously too busy being all moony-eyed over Donny to think up one of her usual mean comments!

A man got up from a canvas chair which had 'Director' on the back and started giving Donny instructions. While they were all waiting for the scene to begin, Tessa spotted a woman with a fat little dog on a lead. It had short fawn-coloured fur, bulging brown eyes and a dark muzzle and wore a collar with 'Lady' in sparkling jewels. The woman doled out doggy choc drops and Lady chomped them all up with a slobbering noise.

Storm licked his lips and gave a hopeful little woof.

Tessa smiled. 'That must be Donny's dog. The way Lady's hoovering up those treats, she'll have scoffed them all in a minute. It looks like Hollywood pooches get the star treatment too, doesn't it?' she whispered to him. 'Don't worry. You won't get left out. I'll get you a treat later.'

Everyone watched in silence as Donny's scene was filmed. He had to say his lines over and over again, while the director shouted, 'Keep rolling!' to the cameras.

The director seemed really strict. Tessa

began to feel nervous and started
fidgeting about.

'Are you all right?' Storm barked
worriedly.

'I'm worried about fluffing my lines,'
Tessa whispered.

'I will help you,' Storm yapped eagerly.

'Thanks, but it's just stage nerves.
Everyone gets them,' Tessa said, smiling.

It was sweet of Storm to offer to help. But what could he do? – after all, he was just a helpless little puppy.

An assistant came up to Tessa and handed her a gold-coloured pocket watch to hold. 'When he tells you to, the director wants you to walk over to Donny and give this to him. OK?' she asked with a kind smile.

Tessa nodded.

'How come *you* get to give Donny the watch?' Kelly complained after the assistant had left. 'I've got more lines than you. It should be me who does it!'

'Don't blame me. I'm just doing what I'm told,' Tessa said, wandering away before an argument started. It hadn't taken long for Kelly to go back to her old self.

'Your boot is undone.' Storm leapt forward and started snapping at Tessa's boot lace, which was trailing on the ground.

'Thanks, Storm, I could have tripped over that,' Tessa said, horrified by the idea of going sprawling in front of everyone.

She found a low wall to sit on and carefully placed the watch beside her before crossing one leg over the other to re-tie the boot.

To her annoyance Kelly dashed over and plonked down on the wall next to her. She really hoped Kelly wasn't going to start teasing her again. But instead Kelly smiled warmly. 'Break a leg, Tessa!' she said, which was something actors often said to each other. It meant good luck for acting in the coming scene.

'Er . . . thanks,' Tessa said, wondering why Kelly was being so friendly all of a sudden.

'See you on the set,' Kelly said abruptly. She got up and hurried away, her long skirts swishing.

Tessa frowned, puzzled. 'What was that all about?' she said to Storm.

'I do not know,' Storm woofed, but he was watching Kelly closely and his midnight-blue eyes were thoughtful.

'The director's almost ready for you. Let's move a bit closer,' Judith told Tessa. 'You'll be on first.'

Tessa's heart began to beat fast. It was a good thing she was still sitting down because her legs had turned to water. 'Oh, I need the pocket watch!' she remembered.

She reached under her skirts and felt
along the top of the wall, where she'd
placed it. But it wasn't there.

Tessa looked all around for the watch.
She checked on the other side of the
wall in case it had fallen over, but there
was no sign of it. 'It has to be here. I
only put it down a minute ago. Oh, this
is awful! The director's going to be
furious!' she cried in dismay.

Storm gazed fixedly at Kelly who was watching Tessa with a smug look on her face. His little muzzle wrinkled in a growl. 'I have an idea where it is!'

Suddenly, Tessa felt a warm tingling sensation flowing down her spine.

Something very strange was about to happen.

Chapter
FOUR

Tessa watched in utter amazement as huge gold sparks ignited in Storm's wavy reddish-brown fur and his ears and tail crackled with electricity. Raising a little front paw he sent a burst of glittery light zooming towards Kelly.

The light divided up into glowing streamers which whizzed up and down and round and round her, as if searching for something. Then, just as if someone had given them a signal, all the streamers shot towards Kelly's dress pocket and disappeared inside. No one else seemed to have noticed anything and Tessa realized that only she could see Storm's magic at work.

Tessa saw Kelly's pocket bulging and

churning as if it was filled with
Mexican jumping beans.

Kelly stiffened. Her eyes widened.
'Ye-ow!' she yelled. Grabbing handfuls
of her skirts, she shook them wildly so
that her pocket tipped open and
something shiny fell out and plopped
on to the grass.

'The watch!' Tessa said, realizing all at
once how Kelly had distracted her
before pinching it off the wall.

Storm gave a triumphant little woof
and then sat down, looking pleased
with himself as every last gold sparkle
faded from his fur.

'Thanks, Storm. Clever old you!' Tessa
whispered, stroking his little head after
quickly checking that no one could see
her doing it.

Kelly stood looking warily down at the watch lying on the floor as if it might jump up and bite her. As Tessa bent down to pick it up, Kelly edged away. 'I wouldn't touch that if I were you. There's something weird about it!' she warned.

'Seems fine to me,' Tessa said, holding the watch. 'How come it was in your pocket anyway?'

'I . . . er . . . saw you drop it. And I was just coming over to give it back to you,' Kelly said.

'Yeah, right,' Tessa said, annoyed. 'That was a really mean trick to play just so I'd get into trouble. I bet you were hoping the director would ask you to give Donny the watch instead. You're just a rotten scene-stealer!'

'I'm not . . . I didn't —' Kelly shouted.

'Quiet on the set!' the director's
annoyed voice interrupted. He glared
at Tessa and Kelly. 'I don't need this.
Someone sort it out. Now!' he
shouted.

Tessa saw Judith striding towards
them with a stern look on her face.
'I thought better of you two. What's
going on? Out with it!' she demanded.

Kelly froze and threw Tessa a scared
look. 'I . . . um. It w-was . . .' she
stammered.

However angry Tessa was, she wasn't a
snitch. She thought quickly. 'I couldn't
find the pocket watch for our scene.
And I got worried that the director
would be cross. Luckily Kelly found it
and she was just giving it back to me.

Sorry. I didn't mean to make so much fuss,' she apologized to Judith.

Kelly's mouth dropped open in shock. 'Um . . . Tessa's . . . right. That's exactly what happened. I'm sorry for getting angry too,' she said.

Judith looked from one to the other. She didn't seem convinced but after a moment she nodded. 'No harm's done, so we'll say no more about this. But please remember that you need to behave yourselves on the set at all times if you want to be taken seriously as actresses.'

'We will,' Tessa said.

'Definitely,' Kelly agreed. When Judith had walked away out of earshot, she grudgingly turned round to Tessa. 'You're not so bad for a spoilt rich kid, Princess.'

'Thanks for nothing!' Tessa murmured, just about managing to control her temper as Kelly walked away.

The final call for her came and Tessa just had time to flutter her fingers in a tiny wave to Storm. Then excitement took over as Tessa prepared for her first ever scene with a major Hollywood star.

'And – action!'

Despite her nerves, Tessa remembered

her lines perfectly. When she stood on the right mark and gave the watch to Donny he winked at her encouragingly. Time seemed to fly and then she had to pretend to be shy and run away.

'And – cut!'

'Thank you, Tessa. Good job,' the director said. He turned to Kelly and Fay and waved to them to come on to the set.

Tessa sat on a chair with Storm on her lap, watching Fay and Kelly act. They were both good but Tessa had goose pimples while Fay was speaking. It was obvious to everyone that the shy girl had something special.

'She just lights up when she's acting,' Tessa said, stroking Storm's silky head. 'I wish I was that good.'

'You are. You just don't see it in yourself,' Storm woofed loyally.

'OK, we're done for now.' The director glanced towards Judith. 'I'll need all the girls back on Thursday afternoon.'

Tessa felt a bit disappointed. Thursday was two whole days away.

Judith smiled as she led them back to wardrobe and make-up. 'Well done. This director doesn't say very much, but I could tell that he was delighted with all of you.'

Later that day when Tessa and Storm were alone, Tessa gave the little puppy a big hug. 'And you were brilliant today too, Storm. I didn't know you could do magic like that! Thanks for getting the gold watch back from Kelly.'

'You are welcome,' Storm barked happily.

After supper, Tessa took Storm for a walk in the grounds. He rushed around, ears flapping, as he investigated the flower beds and sniffed around the trees.

Back in the big house, Tessa phoned
her mum and dad.

They were delighted to hear all about
the scene she had acted in with Donny.
'And how about the other girls? Are
they nice? Have you made friends with
them?' Mrs Churchill asked at the end
of the conversation.

'I have made one brilliant new friend,'
Tessa said, beaming at Storm.

Tessa said her goodbyes and went up to her room. Storm scampered eagerly upstairs beside her.

Fay was sitting on her bed in a pool of light from her reading lamp. She wore a pair of yellow pyjamas with pink teddies and had her diary open on her lap. 'Where's Kelly?' she asked Tessa.

Tessa shrugged. 'I don't know. Maybe she's in the sitting room. Judith and some other people are in there watching a film on TV. It was great today, wasn't it? I really love acting.'

Fay smiled shyly and her hazel eyes sparkled. 'Me too. It wasn't half as bad as I'd expected. I was really dreading it.'

'But you were really good. Everyone

thought so,' Tessa said, surprised. Fay had said her lines perfectly and she'd only had to do them once before the director was satisfied.

'Do you think so?' Fay asked anxiously. 'I always try so hard, but I never think I'm good enough.'

'My dad says that you can't do any more than your best,' Tessa told her. 'That's what I think of when I get stage fright.'

'I'll remember that. Thanks,' Fay said. She got into bed and slipped her diary into her bedside drawer before turning off the lamp. 'Night. See you in the morning, Tessa.'

'Night, Fay.'

Storm leapt on to Tessa's bed and turned round in circles, making himself a soft nest in the duvet. As Tessa got undressed, she smiled to herself. Perhaps she might leave Harpford Manor with more than one new friend after all.

Chapter
FIVE

After lessons the following morning, Judith drove Fay, Kelly and Tessa, with Storm invisibly snuggled up on her lap, into the nearest big town. 'I thought we deserved a treat, and as you're not needed until tomorrow we have plenty of spare time,' she told them.

'I wonder where we're going,' Fay

said to Tessa, as Judith looked for
somewhere to park.

'We'll find out in a minute, won't
we?' Kelly mocked. 'How come you
and Princess are suddenly all buddy-
buddy, anyway?'

'We're not!' Tessa snapped without
thinking and then she noticed Fay's
hurt look. 'I mean, we are kind of . . .

And if you don't stop calling me
"Princess" . . . I won't be responsible!'

'Huh! Who's dented your crown?'
Kelly drawled.

'Look!' Fay called hurriedly as they
passed a cinema. 'Donny Jenton's latest
film is on.'

'I know,' Judith said, grinning. 'That's
where we're going.'

The film was great. It was all about
thieves who are trying to steal a rich
prince's fortune, and had loads of special
effects. Meera Brook, a gorgeous young
actress, was starring with Donny. She
had long dark hair and a tiny waist and
wore fabulous silk gowns.

They all watched the cinema screen
spellbound.

Storm was a bit scared of the loud

noises and flashing lights at first but he soon settled down and enjoyed the film when he realized there was no danger. 'See, Storm, it's all just pretend,' Tessa said soothingly.

Storm took the film very seriously. He growled when Donny's carriage was attacked and woofed excitedly when Donny rescued Meera from a horrible bandit with a bristling beard who was slashing about with a curved sword.

'Oooh, Donny looks mega-lush!' Kelly enthused with a soppy look on her face. 'I wish I was Meera Brook.'

After the film ended, Judith took them all for a pizza. Tessa got

permission to pop into the superstore
which was two doors down. She went
straight to the pet department and
bought a small bag of choc drops and a
dog chew.

Once they all got back to Harpford
Manor, Tessa found a quiet spot in the
grounds to give Storm his treats.

'These taste good,' he woofed, licking his chops.

'Well, I don't see why Lady should be the only pampered dog around here!' Tessa said. 'But if you eat too many you'll soon be a little porker!'

Storm polished off the dog chew too and then flopped on to the grass and rolled on to his back with his tongue lolling out. Tessa smiled as she rubbed his fat rust-coloured tummy. She felt a surge of affection for the gorgeous little pup. 'I wish you could stay with me forever. When I become a famous actress, you can travel everywhere with me.'

Storm rolled on to his front and then stood up and shook himself. 'That is not possible. One day I must return to my own world and lead the Moon–claw pack. Do you understand that, Tessa?' he asked, his midnight–blue eyes wide and serious.

Tessa nodded sadly, but she didn't want to think about that now. She decided to change the subject instead. 'How do you fancy a long walk before I phone Mum and Dad?'

'My favourite thing!' Storm woofed, eagerly wagging his tail.

They went down tree–lined paths and past clipped hedges until they came to a gate leading to an open field with a river at the bottom. Colourful wild flowers nodded in the grass and there was a footpath that seemed to lead to a village in the distance.

Storm lifted his head, his little brown nose twitching. Suddenly, he shot forward like a rocket. 'Rabbits!' he yapped happily.

Tessa smiled as Storm zigzagged after the rabbits, his short, sturdy legs going like pistons. They scattered in all directions and shot down their rabbit holes. Storm didn't seem to mind that they all avoided him easily. He was content with snapping at disappearing white cottontails.

After half an hour, Storm lolloped
over to Tessa, panting heavily, with
his floppy ears flying out behind
him.

Tessa bent down to pat him. 'You
look worn out. I bet you're thirsty
after all that tearing about. Let's go
back and you can have a drink in our
bathroom. It'll be quieter than the
kitchen and no one will notice what
we're doing.'

As they drew near to the main house,
Tessa saw Fay sitting on a bench,
reading *The Stage* newspaper in a patch
of late afternoon sunlight. Tessa waved
to her and Fay waved back.

Tessa and Storm went inside the
manor house and made their way
straight upstairs. As she approached their

room, Tessa heard someone chuckling. 'That sounds like Kelly. What's she up to?'

'I do not know,' Storm yapped suspiciously.

Tessa saw that the older girl was lying on her bed on her tummy. She was reading a thick book with a familiar green cover. 'That's Fay's diary! You shouldn't be reading it!' Tessa exclaimed.

Kelly looked up and started guiltily. 'Oh, it's only you,' she said.

'Put it back in the drawer right now!' Tessa demanded.

'Or what,' Kelly sneered. 'I've got a right to read stuff she's written about me, haven't I? I know she's jealous of me because I've got lots more lines to say and Donny likes me better than you or Fay, I can tell.'

Tessa lunged forward and tried to grab the diary, but Kelly held it out of her reach. 'Stop reading it. It's private,' Tessa said, kneeling on the bed.

Kelly ignored her. 'Listen to this,' she began, reading aloud. '"It's hard to keep up with the others. I always take ages to learn my lines. Everyone else seems to know what to do, but I have to keep asking. They're all better than me at acting."' She sniggered. 'How wet is that?'

'Give me that diary,' Tessa said through clenched teeth.

Kelly sat up. 'Have the stupid thing. It's boring anyway. She hasn't written a single word about me. Catch!' she said, throwing the diary across the room.

It crashed to the floor with a thud and landed heavily on one corner. The cover buckled and twisted and some pages fell out.

'Oops!' Kelly said. 'I'm off. See you!'

She ran out and Tessa heard steps hurrying down the stairs.

Tessa bent down to pick up the diary. 'Look at the state of it now! Fay's going to be so upset.'

'I will help you to mend it,' Storm offered.

Tessa felt another warm tingling feeling trickle down her spine as Storm's rusty-coloured fur lit up with bright gold sparks and his floppy ears glittered with power. A fountain of golden light arched towards the book in Tessa's hands.

Tiny gold sparks like busy worker bees zizzed all over the diary, which squirmed in Tessa's hands as Storm's magic went to work.

Suddenly, footsteps sounded again on

the stairs. 'Tessa, are you in there?' called a voice. 'They've got table tennis. Do you fancy a game?'

'Oh, no! It's Fay!' Tessa whispered desperately.

Chapter SIX

The sparks in Storm's fur instantly went out. Tessa looked down at the diary. It looked worse than before. The cover was all lumps and bumps, one corner was badly dented and even more pages were hanging out.

'I did not have time to finish my magic with Fay so close,' Storm woofed apologetically.

Tessa quickly put the diary behind her back as Fay walked in.

'Hi. I've been looking for —' Fay broke off, looking puzzled, and her smile faded. 'What have you got behind your back?'

Tessa gulped. She knew that Fay would be deeply upset if she found out that Kelly had been reading her private thoughts. She slowly brought her hands forward. 'I . . . um . . . just came in and found this lying on the bed. I was going to put it back in your drawer, but I dropped it and the cover got a bit bashed. Sorry,' she finished lamely.

Fay frowned. 'I *never* leave my diary on my bed.'

'Perhaps you forgot this time?' Tessa suggested.

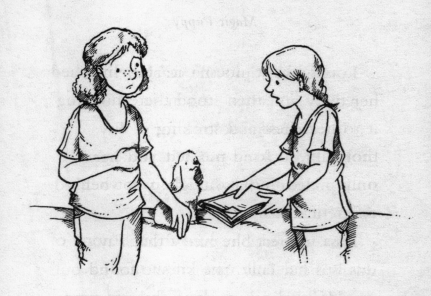

Fay's face darkened. 'No, I didn't.
You've been reading it, haven't you?' she
said in a wavery voice. 'Don't try and
pretend you haven't. I bet you thought
my scribbles were so pathetic that you
kicked my poor diary all round the
room and then jumped on it or
something!'

'I didn't. I wouldn't ever do that!'
Tessa exclaimed.

'Looks like it, doesn't it?' Fay snatched her diary and then stood there hugging it to her chest and stroking it. 'I thought you liked me, but you were only pretending. I thought you were different, Tessa.'

Tessa felt terrible, even though none of this was her fault. She knew that Fay wouldn't believe anything she said now, but she still had to try. 'I *do* like you, Fay. And I didn't read your diary. Honest. Cross my heart and hope to die!'

But Fay wasn't listening any more. She threw herself on to her bed, buried her face in her pillow and curled up with both arms wrapped round the diary.

Sighing heavily, Tessa trudged towards the bathroom.

Storm padded in after her and she closed the door behind him. 'I am sorry. I have made things worse,' he woofed sadly.

Tessa stroked his silky head. 'You were only trying to help. Besides, this is all Kelly's fault.'

Tessa emptied a soap dish and washed it out before pouring water into it for Storm. 'And just when I thought I was starting to get on better with Fay,' she murmured as she watched the tiny puppy lapping thirstily.

The following day it was lessons again and then hours spent in costume and make-up before filming another scene with Donny. This time it was inside Harpford Manor's great hall.

It was a long scene and Tessa had a lot of lines to say. The director was very demanding and bossed everyone about but seemed satisfied with the way things went.

When he called for a coffee break, Tessa decided that she'd go and sit with Fay to have another go at trying to put things right. She passed Kelly, who was sitting munching a bag of crisps.

'I wouldn't bother looking for Fay if I were you,' Kelly said. 'She's gone off somewhere by herself. I bet she's writing more stuff in her soppy old diary.'

'Get knotted, Kelly!' Tessa said crossly, having to make a huge effort not to say something even worse. 'Grrr. Why does

that girl have to be so mean?' she
complained to Storm.

There wasn't time to go searching for
Fay, so Tessa fetched a cold drink and
then sat down with Storm. 'Fay
probably hates me now. I bet she'll

never speak to me again,' she said to him.

'I do not think that anyone could hate you,' Storm woofed, patting her leg with one soft little rusty paw.

'Thanks, Storm.' As Tessa reached down and took hold of the loyal pup's paw, she felt herself starting to calm down. An idea popped into her head. 'Why don't we walk across the field to the village later? Maybe it will have a shop that sells diaries. I can buy Fay a new one!'

Storm nodded. 'I think Fay would like that.'

'She'll probably think I'm just trying to make up with her because I've got a guilty conscience,' Tessa guessed. 'But at least it might make her feel a bit better.'

'You have a very kind heart, Tessa,'
Storm yapped, wagging his tail.

'Try telling Fay that!' Tessa sighed.

The call came for filming to
begin again and the actors began
moving towards the set. Tessa gave
Storm a quick pat and went back to

work, feeling a little better about everything.

'I was proud of you all today,' Judith said to them later as they all ate supper together. 'The director was even more demanding than usual. But you just did as he asked.'

Tessa was feeling really full. She'd asked for another big meal, so that she could share it with Storm. But it was difficult to slip food under the table to him, with everyone talking to her, and she'd had to eat most of it herself.

'I wish we got to see more of Donny,' Kelly commented wistfully. 'I'm his number-one fan, but I haven't even had a chance to ask him for his autograph.'

'He's known to be quite a private person when he's not working,' Judith said.

Fay was picking at her baked potato and salad. After only eating a little, she asked to be excused and left the table.

'Is Fay all right?' Judith asked. 'She's very quiet.'

'She's always like that,' Kelly piped up. 'She's probably just trying to seem interesting and mysterious, like Donny.'

'I think she's still upset because her diary got damaged,' Tessa said, giving Kelly a hard look. She was pleased to see that Kelly looked a tiny bit shamefaced.

'What's that about a diary?' Judith said.

'Oh, the cover got a bit bent, but it's nothing really,' Kelly said. She lowered her voice. 'Some people can't take a joke.'

Tessa stood up before she said something very rude indeed. She wanted to walk over to the village. 'I think I'll go and get some exercise,' she said to Judith as she left the table. 'But first I'll get some ham sandwiches for a snack later.' *At least Storm will have some supper*, she thought.

'Goodness me. Where do you put it all?' Judith said, smiling.

'I've always had a big appetite,' Tessa said hastily, making for the counter.

She took her wrapped package and headed outside with Storm. He scampered after her, his nose twitching at the smell of the ham sandwiches. Once they were by themselves, Tessa broke them into small pieces for him.

Storm chomped them up and then licked his chops. 'Delicious!'

'Ready for an extra-long walk now? As if I need to ask!' Tessa said, grinning.

As they headed towards Harpford

Manor's main gates, they saw some film
equipment stacked up to one side
beside the path. Leaning against it were
some wooden boards painted with
scenery.

Suddenly, a podgy little fawn-coloured
dog with a sparkling collar and a
trailing lead shot through the gateway.
It was Lady!

'She must have run off! Lady! Come
here,' Tessa called in a friendly, gentle
way. But the pug shied away and ran
sideways.

'I will catch her,' Storm yapped
helpfully, bounding forward.

Lady ran headlong towards the
scenery brushing against it as she
looked for a hiding place in this
exciting new game. One of the big

lights that sat right on the top of the stack of film equipment wobbled. It was going to fall!

Tessa looked on in horror as it began to topple towards the ground – with Storm right beneath it!

Chapter
SEVEN

'Look out!' Tessa shouted.

Storm was too intent on snapping at
Lady's trailing lead to notice the danger.
Tessa realized that he wouldn't have
time to use his magical powers.

Without a second thought she threw
herself forward. One step, two steps.
Scoop! Scoop! By a complete miracle
she managed to grab both Storm and

Lady by the scruff of their necks. With
a dog in each hand, she hurtled to one
side as the heavy light crashed down,
missing them all by centimetres.

Tessa stumbled and slipped, twisting
her ankle. 'Oh,' she gasped as a sharp
pain shot through her leg.

Somehow she managed to keep hold

of the two dogs as she collapsed on to the soft grass.

'Thank you for saving me,' Storm woofed, looking subdued as she set him on his feet. 'You were very brave.'

'I'm not really. I couldn't bear anything to happen to you,' Tessa said. She put Lady down too, but kept a firm hold on the pug's lead. As the ache in her ankle increased, she winced.

'You are hurt. I will make you better,' Storm woofed.

Just then Tessa saw a tall figure walking towards the gateway. It was Donny Jenton, completely alone and without his security guards. 'There isn't time. Donny's almost here!' she hissed at Storm.

A familiar warm tingling sensation

flowed down Tessa's spine, but this time there was a rush of backwards movement, just as if she had pressed rewind on her DVD player.

Storm's bright eyes narrowed in concentration as he huffed out a warm puppy breath of tiny gold sparkles. The glittering mist gently swirled round Tessa's sore ankle, sank into it, and she felt the pain fade away completely. There was a sudden jerking movement and Tessa was flicked forward again. She saw that Donny was still the same distance away – no time at all had actually passed!

'Thanks, Storm. That was brilliant. I'm fine now,' she whispered.

'Gruff! Gruff!' Lady barked, trying to wriggle free.

Donny reached out for his dog's lead. 'You're Tessa, aren't you?' he said, his white teeth gleaming as he smiled. 'I saw what you just did. How can I ever thank you for saving Lady?'

'It's no big deal. It just sort of . . . happened,' Tessa said, going red.

'Well, you were very brave. Maybe a little dumb too, to risk getting squashed

by that heavy light. I don't think your parents would approve. But don't worry, I won't tell anyone,' Donny said with a twinkle in his eye.

He gave Lady a cuddle. 'Bad girl. Why did you take off like that?' he scolded, wagging his finger as Lady snuffled and licked his nose.

'Maybe she wanted a good long run off her lead,' Tessa suggested. 'She probably gets bored just sitting around and being fed treats. And I hope you don't mind me saying, but she's a bit overweight.'

Donny raised his eyebrows. 'Really? Why hasn't anyone else told me that?'

Tessa wisely decided not to answer.

Donny put Lady down on the floor.

'Let's get you back. From now on, you're going to get a lot *more* exercise and the choccy drops are history!' He looked at Tessa. 'Thanks again, honey. Can I give you a lift back up the drive to the front door? My driver's parked just down the road.'

'Thanks, but I've got some shopping to do. I think I'm still going to go into the village,' Tessa said.

'Well, OK. Isn't there anything I can do for you? I'd like to show my appreciation for the way you saved Lady,' Donny said.

'No, I don't think . . .' Tessa paused as an idea jumped into her mind. 'Well, maybe there is something . . .'

Donny listened as Tessa explained her idea and then he grinned. 'I'd be delighted. How about after filming finishes tomorrow? My driver will pick you up.' He gave Tessa a quick wave as he set off with Lady puffing noisily beside him.

As Tessa had hoped, there was a newsagent's shop in the village.

She did her shopping and then decided to return to Harpford Manor along the footpath that ran across the field. Storm trotted at Tessa's heel, his nose to the ground as he snuffled about. The trip had been a success and Tessa now carried a bag containing a brand-new diary, covered in shiny green plastic. It even had a strap with a heart-shaped padlock and a key to lock it with.

'I really hope this cheers Fay up — even just a little bit,' she said, glancing down at Storm.

But he seemed to have run off.

'Storm? Where are you?' Tessa called.

She looked across the field, expecting to see him chasing rabbits, but there was no sign of him. Puzzled, she circled round, scanning the field more carefully, and just spotted the tip of Storm's rusty-coloured tail as he dived into the bottom of a hedgerow.

She hurried over. 'What's this hide and seek —' she began and then stopped as she realized that Storm was trembling all over. She bent down and looked through the tangled branches at him. 'What's wrong?'

'Shadow has found me! He has put a spell on those dogs!' Storm whined in terror, his midnight-blue eyes wide and fearful.

'What dogs, Storm?' Tessa looked up. In the next field a man with two black-and-white sheepdogs was herding some sheep into a pen. The dogs were running back and forth and snapping at the sheep's heels.

'I don't *think* those dogs are after you. But how can I tell if they're under a magic spell?' Tessa asked Storm.

Storm whimpered and burrowed deeper into the hedgerow. 'They will have pale cold eyes and extra-long teeth. And be very fierce and strong.'

Tessa looked hard at the sheepdogs, which were following their owner's orders closely. 'They don't look like that. I think they're OK. But you've had a nasty fright. Let's get back,' Tessa said.

Storm squirmed towards her and she bent down and reached for the terrified puppy. As Tessa set off again with Storm in her arms, she felt his little heart fluttering against her hand. The glimpse of possible danger reminded Tessa again that Storm might have to leave suddenly in order to save himself.

She felt a pang as she realized that however much she might try to prepare herself for losing Storm she would never be ready to let him go.

Chapter
EIGHT

The moment Tessa and Storm reached
Harpford Manor, they set off to find
Fay and give her the new diary. Tessa
checked the sitting room and the games
room before she finally tracked her
down in their bedroom.

Fay was reading a book. She looked
up as Tessa came in and gave her a
small smile.

Tessa felt encouraged. At least Fay seemed willing to talk. 'Good book?' she asked hopefully.

Fay nodded. 'It's fairy stories, with really great illustrations. See? Ogres, goblins and monsters, and there's a handsome prince who rescues a beautiful princess from a swamp monster.'

'Sounds exciting,' Tessa said, even though she didn't think she'd fancy reading it herself. She went and peered over Fay's shoulder. 'The prince looks a bit like Donny. Don't show it to Kelly or she'll get drool all over the page!'

Fay giggled. 'Tessa. I wanted to talk to –' she began shyly.

'OK, but me first,' Tessa said quickly,

thrusting the plastic bag at Fay. 'I got
you this. I hope you like it.'

'For me?' Fay's eyes widened as she
reached inside the bag and took out
the shiny new diary. 'Oh, it's brilliant!
And it locks too. Look at this cute little
key.'

'Yes. So no one can read your diary
now,' Tessa said. 'Look, about the other
evening. I know you probably still
won't believe that I didn't read —'

'But I do believe you!' Fay broke in excitedly. 'That's what I was about to tell you just now. I came in here and caught Kelly reading my diary earlier and she admitted everything. She couldn't even be bothered to lie. Anyway, I know that you had nothing to do with what happened.'

Tessa took a second or two to let this sink in. 'Good. So . . . um . . . we can be friends now?'

'If you still want to,' Fay said, her hazel eyes sparkling. 'And thanks loads for my new diary. I love it to bits.'

'You're welcome,' Tessa said, beaming. 'And guess who I just saw on the way to the village when I went to buy it. Donny Jenton!'

'Really? Did he have heaps of

bodyguards with him?' Fay asked.

'No. He was all by himself. He was looking for Lady, who'd escaped and run away.' Tessa told Fay about dashing after Lady and almost getting flattened by the heavy light but she missed out all mention of Storm. 'Donny was so pleased that Lady was safe that he offered me a reward. At first I couldn't think of anything I wanted. But then I asked if he'd take me and my friends out for a burger or something.'

'You didn't!' Fay said, deeply impressed. 'What did he say?'

Tessa smiled. 'He was dead keen. He's arranging for his car to pick us up after we finish filming tomorrow.'

'Wow! That's so cool!' Fay exclaimed.

'Wait until Kelly hears about this!'

'Hears about what?' Kelly demanded from the open doorway. 'As if I'd be interested in any of your pathetic plans!'

'So you don't want to hear about how Fay and me are going out for a burger with Donny tomorrow evening?' Tessa said casually.

'What? Don't make me laugh!' Kelly said. 'Soppy old Fay and silly, spoilt Princess going on a date with Donny? As if!'

Tessa kept hold of her temper. She shrugged. 'Well, you'll see for yourself, won't you? When Donny sends his car for us.'

'Yeah, right!' Kelly crowed, but she didn't look so sure of herself now. 'Why would he want to take you two muppets anywhere?'

'Because Tessa saved Lady from getting squashed when some equipment almost fell on her,' Fay said. 'Isn't that right, Tessa?'

Tessa nodded. 'Donny's *my* number-one fan now. I might get his autograph for you, if you ask me really, really

nicely!' she teased Kelly and was pleased to see the older girl flush with jealousy. She turned to Fay. 'Fancy a game of table tennis?'

'You bet!' Fay cried, linking arms with Tessa. They swanned past Kelly with Storm trotting invisibly after them.

'I don't believe a word of it. You're just a zonking great fibber, Tessa Churchill!' Kelly shouted after them.

'Am I? We'll see,' Tessa replied smugly.

Halfway down the stairs Tessa and Fay clapped their hands over their mouths and started to laugh. 'Did you see the look on her face? You are *so* bad!' Fay whispered through her fingers.

'I couldn't help it!' Tessa answered. 'I really enjoyed getting my own back for once. Besides, Kelly won't be left out for long. I'll tell her tomorrow that she's invited to come with us!'

Tessa held up her long skirts as she emerged from wardrobe in full costume the following morning. 'I can't believe that this is my last day of filming. It's gone by so fast!' she whispered to Storm.

Storm nodded, his midnight-blue eyes looking a little troubled.

'Are you looking forward to coming home with me? Mum and Dad are going to love you,' Tessa said.

But Storm didn't answer. She noticed that he kept glancing nervously around as he followed Tessa down to the big old-fashioned kitchen where the scene was being filmed. 'Is something wrong?' she asked him.

'Shadow is very close now. I can feel it. He will use his magic to make any dogs nearby hunt me down,' the terrified puppy whined, beginning to tremble like a leaf.

'Oh, no!' Tessa gasped, going cold all over. 'Maybe it's another false alarm.'

Storm shook his head. 'Not this time.'

Tessa racked her brains, trying to think of what to do. 'I know! How about hiding among the costumes? There are thousands of them. It would be hard for any dogs to find you in there. As soon as I've finished this scene, I'll come and fetch you.'

'It is a good plan,' Storm agreed. He set off, ears and tail flying.

Somehow Tessa followed the director's instructions and remembered all her lines. The second she was free, she hared off towards wardrobe.

As Tessa reached it, Storm shot towards her in terror, ducking into a side room. There were three mongrel dogs hard on his heels. They had pale eyes and extra-long teeth and were growling fiercely.

Tessa's heart missed a beat. Her plan hadn't worked! Storm was in terrible danger.

She rushed after the tiny puppy and fierce enemy dogs just as a dazzling flash of gold light stopped her in her tracks. When the light faded, Tessa rubbed the sparkles from her eyes to see that Storm stood there, a helpless puppy no longer, but his true magnificent wolf self. An older female wolf with a gentle face stood next to him.

Tessa realized that the moment she had been dreading was here. She was going to have to be very brave. 'Go! Save yourself, Storm!' she cried, her voice breaking.

Storm's midnight-blue eyes shone

with affection, and gold dust glimmered in his thick silver-grey neck-ruff. 'Be of good heart, Tessa. You have been a true friend,' he said in a velvety growl.

There was a final bright gold flash and Storm and his mother began to fade before disappearing forever. The mongrel dogs leapt forward, but they were too late. Their eyes and teeth instantly returned to normal and they slunk out.

Tessa gulped. It had all happened so fast. She felt stunned. 'I'll never forget you, Storm,' she whispered as tears pricked her eyes.

Tessa had just finished drying her eyes when Fay popped her head into the room. 'I've been looking for you. It's almost five thirty. We have to get out of these costumes before we go and meet Donny. I've just told Kelly that we're *all* going for a burger. You should have seen her face!'

'I bet it was priceless,' Tessa said, smiling despite herself.

As she went with Fay, Tessa felt herself beginning to get excited again at the thought of meeting up with Donny Jenton – she knew so many people who would give anything to be in her place.

But whatever the future held, Tessa
knew that her secret magic puppy
friend, Storm, would always be the true
star of her life.

I have big

Hk Plays a woof

is

or is I-Lee

Hk

I have fan
my puppy
hr name
is priss. I love
her

Magic Puppy

Party Dreams

magic puppy

I have.
a Damashin

She is named
Stone I love
her.

Prologue

The young silver-grey wolf bounded towards the stream that ran through the snow-covered valley. Dipping his head, Storm lapped at the clear icy water. It felt good to be home again.

Suddenly, a terrifying howl rose in the still air.

'Shadow!' Storm gasped. The fierce lone wolf who had attacked Storm's pack and left his mother wounded was very close.

In an instant, there was a bright gold flash and the young silver-grey wolf disappeared. Where Storm had been standing there was now a tiny spotted Dalmatian puppy with a pink muzzle, a wet black nose and huge midnight-blue eyes.

Storm's puppy heart beat fast and he started to tremble as he hoped this disguise would protect him. He must find somewhere to hide — and quickly.

There was a clump of snow-covered bushes some way upstream. Storm ran towards them, almost tripping over his own paws as they skidded on the hard snow. He was just about to leap into the bushes, when he saw the dark shape of an adult wolf crouching beneath them.

Storm gasped. Shadow was waiting to ambush him! It was too late to run. This was the end.

The adult wolf lifted its head.

'Storm! In here, quickly!'

'Mother!' Storm sighed with relief as he recognized the gentle face of the she-wolf.

He scrambled into the bushes, his body wriggling and his short thin tail wagging a greeting. Canista rumbled affectionately as she licked her disguised cub's smooth spotted fur. 'It is good to see you, my son,' she growled softly. 'But you cannot stay. Shadow wants to lead the Moon-claw pack, but the others will not follow him while you live. It is too dangerous for you right now.'

Storm growled and his midnight-blue eyes sparked with anger and fear. 'Shadow killed my father and three litter brothers, but he will not lead our pack. I will face him and fight him!'

Canista nodded. 'One day you will, Storm. But you are still too small and I am weak from Shadow's poisoned bite and cannot help you. Use this disguise. Go back to the other world and return when you are stronger.' As she stopped speaking, her eyes clouded with pain.

Storm whined with sympathy. He huffed out a puppy breath filled with tiny gold sparks. They swirled around Canista's injured paw, before sinking into her fur and disappearing.

'Thank you. The pain is easing,' Canista sighed gratefully.

Suddenly, a dark shadow fell across the bush where Storm and his mother were hiding. Iron-hard paws scrabbled at the packed snow as the fierce wolf came closer.

'Come out, Storm! Let us end this now!' Shadow challenged.

'Go! Save yourself!' Canista urged.

Storm whimpered and his big blue eyes widened as he felt the power building inside his little body. Glittering sparks ignited in his smooth spotted fur. The golden light around him grew brighter. And brighter . . .

Chapter
ONE

Paige Riley sat sulking in the back of her step-dad's car. It wasn't fair. She'd been right in the middle of talking about birthday parties with her two best friends, when Keith called to collect her.

'Why couldn't Mum pick me up, like we'd arranged? Then I could have stayed another hour with Amy and Tori,'

Paige complained. 'Mum knows we always get excited because our birthdays all come so close together.'

'I'm sorry, love. I didn't want to say anything until we were by ourselves, but your mum's been taken into hospital,' Keith explained as he pulled away from the kerb. 'They've done tests and she and the baby are both fine, but she's going to have to stay in hospital and rest until he's born.'

Paige was glad it was nothing serious. 'Poor Mum. She hates hospitals. She won't like being stuck in there for weeks. It's a good thing half-term holidays start tomorrow. I'll be able to go and visit her every day and cheer her up.'

Keith glanced at her in the rear-view

mirror. 'Well, maybe not *every* day. I'm
on nights for the next two weeks. So
your mum and I think it's best if you
stay with my mum for the time being.'

Paige wrinkled her nose. She'd never
met Keith's mum, but she knew that
she lived in a village out in the middle
of nowhere. 'Do I have to? Can't I stay
in town with Granny and Gramps
Riley instead?' she asked.

'I'm afraid not. They're on holiday,'
Keith explained. 'I know Brookton
village is a bit remote, but I'll come
over and fetch you when I can and
take you to see your mum. By the
way, try not to call my mother Gran
or Nan, will you? She's a bit sensitive
about her age.'

'What shall I call her then?'

'Her name's Deborah. She likes
everyone to call her Debs,' Keith said.

Paige snorted. Debs! What sort of
name was that for a step-gran? 'Anyway,
I don't need to go and stay with
anyone else. I can look after myself in
our flat. I'm not a baby. I'll be ten in
two weeks.'

Keith smiled. 'I know. And you're a
very grown-up sensible young lady. But

I don't like the idea of you being left by yourself all day *and* all night. Besides, your mum will feel happier knowing that you'll be taken care of. We can't have anything worrying her at a time like this, can we?' he said reasonably.

There was no answer to that. Paige knew when she was beaten. 'But what about my things? I need my jeans and trainers and —'

'I've already packed a case for you,' Keith interrupted. 'I can get anything else you want later. All right?'

Paige nodded miserably, her shoulders drooping. It wasn't all right. It was all wrong! This new baby had somehow managed to spoil things for her before he was even born! She probably wouldn't even be able to have a birthday party.

Her heart sank as she thought of Amy and Tori, who would still be planning their parties and deciding what to wear. There was no point in her joining in now.

Keith drove through town and out on to a country road. After what seemed like hours, he turned down a dark twisty lane and stopped in front of a large detached red-brick house. There was a light on in the porch and just as Paige reached the front door it creaked open.

A woman with tied-back dark hair, a flowing velvet top and jeans swooped out in a cloud of perfume. 'Hello, you must be Paige. Come in, darling. I'm

really looking forward to getting to
know you.'

Paige smiled stiffly, wishing she could
say the same. 'Thanks for letting me stay
with you, Mrs Stokes,' she said politely.

'Oh, call me Debs — everyone does,'
Debs said, beaming as she ushered Paige
into the house.

Paige stared at the coloured floor tiles
and stained-glass windows. Old-fashioned
glass wall lamps cast a dim glow over the
rich wallpaper and dark paintwork. The
house was like something out of a
creepy ghost story. Paige wouldn't have
been surprised to see giant bats hanging
upside down from the ceiling.

Keith took her case upstairs and then
came into the kitchen where Debs was
filling the kettle. 'I'll get straight off

then. They're expecting me back at work. Will you be OK, Paige?' he asked.

Paige nodded uneasily. She wasn't OK really. She hated this gloomy house and she didn't know what to make of Debs but she wasn't about to say so in front of everyone.

'I hope you'll be happy staying with me in my funny old house, even though I know that you must be

longing to be at home with your gorgeous new baby brother,' Debs said, smiling warmly.

You couldn't be more wrong, Paige thought, but she wisely stayed silent.

After Keith left, having promised to phone the following day, Debs made hot chocolate. As they sat drinking it, Paige stifled a yawn.

'You look worn out. This is all a bit sudden, isn't it? Come on, I'll show you your bedroom. Bring your drink with you,' Debs said kindly.

Paige trudged upstairs behind Debs. Her bedroom had the same rich wallpaper, dark paintwork and heavy furniture as the rest of the house. Paige blinked at the enormous four-poster bed that stood against one wall.

'Impressive, isn't it? That bed's been
in the family for donkey's years. I was
born in it and so was Keith,' Debs said
cheerily.

Yuck! Too much information, Paige
thought. 'I'd like to go to sleep now,
please,' she said hurriedly.

'Of course you would, darling. It's
been a long day. Sweet dreams. I'll see

you in the morning.' Debs closed the door behind her.

Paige quickly undressed and brushed her teeth at the big old-fashioned basin before climbing into the vast bed. She lay there shivering. Moonlight poured in through the curtains, casting shadows and making the dark furniture into lumpish shapes.

Her tummy felt all tight and churning. A wave of loneliness washed over her. She wished her mum didn't have to stay in hospital. This was all her baby brother's fault.

Suddenly, a dazzling flash of bright light lit up the whole room and Paige gasped as her sad thoughts disappeared with the darkness. She rubbed her eyes in disbelief – at the bottom of the bed

seemed to be sitting a tiny figure,
glowing with thousands of diamond
points of light.

'Aargh! A ghost!' Paige gave a
strangled scream and dived under the
covers.

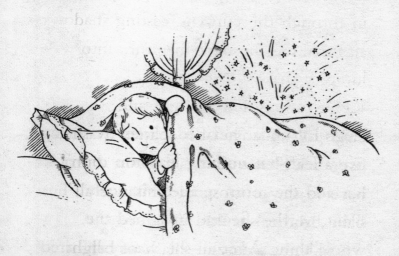

Chapter
TWO

Paige lay under her bed covers trembling like a leaf, but nothing leapt on top of her and the room seemed strangely silent. Maybe she had imagined the whole thing. After all she was really tired and not feeling like herself at all.

Very slowly, Paige lowered the covers and peeped over the top of them. 'Oh!' she gasped.

To her complete amazement a tiny cute puppy with black spots on a smooth white coat and the brightest midnight-blue eyes she had ever seen was sitting on the bed.

Was it a ghost dog? Whatever it was, it wasn't glowing any more. In fact, it was blinking at her and wagging its slim spotty tail. Paige found herself smiling as her heartbeat began to return to

normal. She sat up properly and leaned back against the pillows.

'Hello! Aren't you gorgeous? I didn't know that Debs had a Dalmatian puppy!' She rubbed her fingers together encouragingly, hoping that the puppy wanted to make friends.

To her delight, it padded up the bed towards her and she felt its slight weight as it climbed on to her legs.

'I am sorry if I startled you,' the puppy woofed.

Paige did a double take and snatched back her hand. Maybe it was a ghost puppy after all! 'How come y-you can s-speak?' she stammered.

'Where I come from, all of my pack can speak,' the puppy yapped. Despite being so tiny it didn't seem to be too afraid of her. 'I am Storm of the Moon-claw pack. Who are you?'

Paige still couldn't believe this was really happening, but her curiosity was getting the better of her fear. She watched warily as Storm lay down on the old-fashioned bedspread and then put his head on one side as if expecting an answer.

'I'm Paige. Paige Riley. I'm staying in this spooky old house because my mum's in hospital resting until my baby brother's born,' she found herself explaining. 'My step-dad can't look after me in our flat because he has to work.'

'I am honoured to meet you, Paige,' Storm woofed, bowing his head.

Paige hardly dared to move in case she frightened this amazing puppy away.

She noticed that Storm was beginning
to tremble all over.

'Are you OK?' Paige couldn't imagine
why he might be afraid of *her*.

'I need to hide. Can you help me?'
he whined.

Paige frowned. 'Who are you hiding
from? Is someone after you?'

Storm's bright blue eyes flashed with
anger and fear. 'Yes, a fierce lone wolf

called Shadow, who attacked my father
and litter brothers and wounded my
mother. Now he wants to lead the
Moon-claw pack, but the others want
me for their leader.'

Paige listened in amazement. 'But
how can you lead a wolf pack? You're
just a pup—' she began.

'I will show you!' Storm barked.

He jumped up and leapt off the bed
on to the thick carpet. There was
another dazzling bright gold flash, so
bright that Paige was blinded for a
moment.

'Oh!' she rubbed her eyes and when
she could see again she realized that the
cute Dalmatian puppy had disappeared.
In its place, there stood a magnificent
young silver-grey wolf.

Paige eyed the young wolf's sharp
teeth, muscular legs and huge paws that
seemed too big for his body. As he
shook himself, gold sparks danced out
of his thick fur. 'Storm?' she said,
inching back under the covers.

'Yes, it is me. Do not be afraid. I will
not harm you,' Storm rumbled in a
soft growl.

But before Paige had time to get used
to seeing Storm as his impressive real
self, a last flare of intense gold light
filled the gloomy bedroom and Storm
reappeared before her as a helpless little
Dalmatian puppy.

'Wow! You really are a wolf. No one
would ever guess,' Paige said, deeply
impressed by Storm's disguise.

'Shadow will not be fooled if he finds

me. I need to hide now.' Storm gave a little whimper of fear as he began trembling all over again.

Paige's soft heart went out to him. With his smooth spotted fur, alert little face and huge glowing blue eyes, Storm was the most gorgeous puppy she had ever seen. 'Why don't you jump back up here and stay with me tonight?' she suggested. 'This bed's so enormous that half my school could hide in it. We can think about what else to do in the morning.'

Storm gave her a doggy grin and then leapt back up on to the bed, trailing gold sparks behind him like a tiny comet. 'That is a good plan!'

Paige made a cosy bed for Storm by fluffing up a spare pillow.

'Thank you, Paige,' Storm woofed. He jumped on to the pillow and circled round and round before finally settling down. Tucking his nose between his little spotted front paws, he gave a contented sigh. 'This is a safe place.'

'Yes, but it's still very dark in here,' Paige said, trying not to sound too nervous.

Storm lifted his head again. Gold specks twinkled in his spotty fur and a soft glow spread outwards from him, lighting up the room. 'Is that better?'

'Much! Thanks, Storm.' Paige lay down and snuggled under the covers. The four-poster bed didn't seem so vast and lonely any more.

Maybe staying with Debs in this gloomy old house wouldn't be quite so bad now that she had Storm for a friend. As Paige and Storm fell asleep, the gentle glow filled every shadowy corner and just stopped short of spilling out under the door.

Chapter
THREE

'Rise and shine, darling!' Deborah Stokes poked her head round the bedroom door the following morning. 'Goodness me. Where did that puppy come from? Keith didn't say anything about you bringing a pet!'

Paige woke instantly. She sat up, rubbing her eyes. Oh no. She must have overslept!

Storm was just waking up too. He stretched his front paws out and yawned, showing a pink tongue and sharp little white teeth.

Debs put her hands on her hips. Her hair was loose on her shoulders and she was wearing a black kimono with big red poppies all over it. 'I'm waiting. I think you owe me an explanation, young lady,' she said sternly.

Paige gulped. 'You're never going to believe this, but Storm's here because he's hiding from his evil enemy. And guess what. He can ta–' she began excitedly, but Storm suddenly reached over and tapped her cheek with one tiny spotty front paw.

'Wroo-oof! Wroo-oof!' he said loudly, looking up at her with pleading midnight-blue eyes and shaking his head.

Paige looked at Storm, confused, before realizing that the tiny puppy didn't want her to tell Debs about him. She patted him reassuringly, letting him know that she understood.

'What's wrong with him? Why's he making that noise?' Debs asked, puzzled.

'Um . . . I think Storm just woke up with a bit of a jolt. He was probably in the middle of a dream or something . . .' Paige improvised hastily. She began wracking her brains for something more convincing to tell Debs that would protect Storm's secret. 'Sorry, I got a bit carried away. What I meant to say was that I'm . . . er, looking after Storm for a . . . friend. But I haven't told Mum or Keith about it. I was going to hide him in my bedroom at the flat, but then Mum was taken to hospital and I had to come here. Storm was in my . . . um . . . shoulder bag when Keith drove me here last night and I smuggled him upstairs. I just really want him to stay! I was going to buy dog food with my pocket money,' she fibbed.

'Hmm,' Debs said doubtfully. 'Why can't your friend look after her own puppy?'

'Oh, she can . . . when . . . when she gets back from her holiday,' Paige rushed on, thinking that this was getting very complicated. 'But pets aren't allowed in their hotel and all the boarding kennels were full. That's why I said I'd look after him.'

Debs stood for a moment in silence before reaching out to stroke Storm. Storm looked up at her with big dewy eyes and gave a little whine. He wagged his tail and licked her hand.

Paige had to smile at his 'Please-like-me-and-let-me-stay' act.

It worked. Debs's face softened. 'He's certainly a cute little chap and he seems friendly, but I hadn't banked on having a puppy around. I'm very proud of my garden. I really don't want him digging up holes in my flowerbeds and burying bones.'

'Oh, he wouldn't do that!' Paige promised. 'I'll make sure Storm behaves himself. Please say that he can stay with me. And . . . and you won't tell Keith

about this, will you?' she asked in her best pleading voice. 'I'll be grounded for at least a year!'

Debs looked at her sternly and then a big grin stole over her face. 'You're a cheeky minx and no mistake! But I admire people who show initiative. All right, Storm can stay. And he'll be our secret.'

'Really? That's brilliant! Thanks *so* much,' Paige cried. 'I'll look after him really well. You'll hardly notice he's here.'

Debs nodded. 'See that you do,' she said firmly, her eyes twinkling.

Downstairs, Debs cooked them all a breakfast of sausages, eggs and toast. She even let Paige give Storm two sausages,

cut into tiny pieces. 'But only until we get some proper dog food. I don't want him being sick on my antique carpets,' she commented.

Paige thought that you'd hardly notice, they were so covered in swirls and patterns, but she wisely kept silent. After they finished eating, she took Storm into the garden to have a little run around.

'I'm actually starting to quite like Debs,' she said, wandering after him in case any of Debs's flowers got trampled by little paws. 'She seems strict, but she's kind too.'

'I like her as well,' Storm woofed in agreement and then his little face turned serious. 'Thank you for not telling her my secret. You can never tell anyone; promise me, Paige.'

Paige felt disappointed. She thought Storm might say this but had secretly been hoping she could tell Amy and Tori all about her magical new friend. They would think this was so cool! Paige was prepared to do whatever it took to keep Storm safe though. 'OK. I promise. No one's going to hear about you from me — ever!'

Storm wrinkled his little pink muzzle
and black nose, rolled his lips back and
showed his teeth. Paige blinked, worried
that Storm was snarling. But he wasn't
making growling noises. Why was he
doing that?

Storm looked surprised at himself.
He did it again. 'Oh, this is how I show
that I am pleased. It is a smile. It is
something special that Dalmatian dogs
do,' he yapped.

Paige felt a laugh bubbling up inside her, but she didn't want to hurt his feelings. Storm looked as cute as could be, sitting there practising his Dalmatian grin.

A moment later he shot across the lawn to chase some leaves that were whirling about in the breeze.

Paige watched him affectionately. She loved having Storm all to herself and not having to share him with anyone.

Chapter
FOUR

Keith came over to pick Paige up that afternoon before he went to the factory. 'I thought you'd like to visit your mum,' he said. 'It might cheer her up. She's already bored with having to rest in bed.'

Paige smiled. She'd known she would be.

'How are you and Debs getting on?'

Keith asked anxiously as they stood in the hall.

'Fine,' Paige said, shrugging. 'I don't even mind staying with her, as long as it's not for too long.'

Keith looked pleased. 'I'm glad, Paige. That'll be a big relief for your mum, and I really think Debs is enjoying your company.'

He ruffled her short brown hair

fondly and went off to have a quick chat with Debs, while Paige went upstairs to get ready.

Paige found Storm dozing on her bed. With the autumn sunlight pouring through the window on to him, his dark spots really showed up against his smooth white fur. He opened one bright blue eye and wagged his tail as Paige bent over him.

'Will you be OK here all by yourself until I get back from town?' she asked.

Storm's other eye snapped open and he sprang up on to his paws. 'I will come with you!' he woofed eagerly.

Paige smiled and stroked the top of his silky head. 'I'd love you to. But what if Keith sees you? Besides, I don't think puppies are allowed in hospitals.'

'I will use my magic so that no one but you will be able to see and hear me,' Storm told her.

'You can make yourself invisible? Cool! There's no problem then. Maybe you should still get into my shoulder bag? You'll be safer in there until we get to the hospital.'

Paige unzipped her bag and Storm jumped in and settled down on top of her woolly gloves. After brushing her hair and pulling on a fleece body warmer, Paige picked up her bag and went downstairs to where Keith was waiting.

They said goodbye to Debs and then headed for the hospital. Paige suggested they stop on the way to buy some magazines. 'Mum likes the celebrity gossip ones,' she told him.

'Good idea. I'll get her some flowers too,' Keith said.

At the hospital, he showed Paige down the maze of corridors to the maternity ward. Paige spotted her mum right away. She was sitting up on the second bed from the entrance.

Mrs Riley's eyes lit up when she saw Keith and Paige. She looked flushed and pretty in a new blue nightdress and matching dressing gown.

Paige rushed over to give her mum a hug and a kiss, delighted to see her looking well.

'Ooh, flowers *and* magazines. Lovely. You two are spoiling me!' her mum exclaimed.

Paige sat down on the visitor's chair beside the bed. 'You deserve to be spoiled, Mum. Are you OK?'

'I'm a bit tired, but that's all. I feel like a bit of a fraud staying in here actually,' her mum replied, pulling a face. She patted her round tummy. 'I'll be glad when this little man makes his appearance!'

Paige chose not to say anything. She slipped her bag off her shoulder to put it on the floor and saw Storm jump out and go gambling off down the ward. He had his head down, and his tail was wagging as he snuffed up the interesting smells. Even though Paige knew that the tiny spotty puppy was invisible to everyone else, she still expected a nurse or someone to notice him. But when nothing happened, she began to relax. Storm was much less trouble than a baby brother was going to be!

'I'll go and see if I can find a vase to put these flowers in. You girls can have a good old natter,' Keith said.

'He's being tactful,' Mrs Riley commented. 'I hope it's not too awful in that loopy old house with Debs. She

used to be an actress, you know. And she still dresses like one! Is she bossing you around or anything? Just let me know and I'll have a word with her.'

Paige grinned at the determined look on her mum's face. 'Debs has actually been really nice to me and St—' She stopped herself quickly, realizing that she would have to be a lot more careful about keeping Storm's secret. 'But I'm not keen on all her antique stuff. You should see the monster bed I'm sleeping in! It's as big as the entire kitchen in our flat!'

'Well, don't get used to having all that space to yourself,' her mum said, laughing. 'You'll have to go back to your ordinary poky old bedroom.'

'I like my bedroom being small. It's

cosy,' Paige said. 'But I can put up with staying away from home for a little bit longer, I guess.'

'Well, I'm glad you're making the best of things. Don't say anything to Keith, but I was worried that you'd feel a bit lonely and cut off over in Brookton, what with Debs having no car.'

'Oh, I'll manage,' Paige said. *I'm not lonely, now that I've got Storm for my friend*, she thought. She could see him sniffing around under the bed opposite. Her lips twitched as she imagined the look on her mum's face if she knew there was an invisible puppy a few metres away!

Mrs Riley reached out and took Paige's hand. 'I'm sorry that your birthday's going to be a bit of a non-event with me in here. Keith obviously can't manage a party with the hours he's working. You don't mind too much, do you, pet?'

Paige minded very much. She swallowed. 'No problem, Mum. There's always next year,' she said, trying hard to hide her disappointment.

'That's my lovely sensible good girl. I knew you'd understand,' her mum said, fondly squeezing her hand. 'Once I get

home we'll have some serious girl time all to ourselves; all right?'

Paige nodded, but she couldn't make herself believe it. The lady in the flat next door had a baby. It hardly seemed to sleep at all and when it was awake it was crying to be fed or changed.

A lump rose in her throat as she wished that she could have her mum all to herself again, like before she met Keith and before a baby half-brother was on its way. Paige felt a pang as she realized that she wasn't ready to get into the big sister thing.

'Had a good chat, you two?' Keith said, putting the vase of flowers on top of the bedside cabinet.

Paige nodded and managed a wobbly smile. While her mum and Keith were talking, she leafed through one of her mum's magazines. Storm padded over, lay down and rested his front paws on one of her trainers.

'Is something wrong?' he woofed.

Paige checked that no one was listening before she replied. 'I'm just feeling a bit fed up, that's all,' she whispered.

'Can I do anything to help?' Storm offered.

Paige shook her head. 'No one can.' But as she looked into his bright midnight-blue eyes, she felt herself cheering up a bit. At least Storm was here just for her.

Keith dropped Paige and Storm at Debs's house and then left for work

straightaway. There was a note from
Debs in the kitchen, saying that she was
at her book group at a friend's house
down the road and wouldn't be long.
She'd scribbled a phone number too, if
Paige needed it.

Paige got herself a drink and forked
some dog food into a bowl for Storm.
Storm chomped it up and then sat
back, licking his chops. He trotted over
to the table where Paige was sitting,
staring glumly into her orange juice.

'You are very quiet, Paige,' he woofed,
his blue eyes clouding with concern.

Paige sighed heavily. 'I was thinking
about not having a birthday party this
year. It's not fair. And I don't even
know what to do about Amy and Tori.
I know they'd understand about Mum

being in hospital. But I'd feel really weird about going to their parties, if they can't come to mine. Maybe I should just phone and say that I'm not coming.'

'Then your friends would be upset too,' Storm woofed.

Paige realized that he was right. 'I wouldn't want that. OK, maybe I'll still go. Amy's is on Friday. That's only the day after tomorrow and I haven't got her a present yet. I should have got her one while I was with Keith. Now it's too late. The buses into town from here only run about once every ten years!'

Storm's midnight-blue eyes lit up with purpose. 'I will help. Put me down, please.'

Paige did so. She frowned as she felt

a strange warm tingling sensation flowing down her spine as bright gold sparks began igniting in Storm's smooth spotty fur.

Something very unusual was about to happen.

Chapter
FIVE

Paige watched in complete amazement as the sparks in Storm's fur grew brighter and brighter and his ears crackled and popped with electricity. A glowing gold light spread around them both. It began forming into a long glittery tube that suddenly whooshed through the kitchen window.

Paige stared at the shining rainbow-shaped tube as it seemed to come to rest somewhere in the region of the town. In the middle of Debs's kitchen, there was now an entrance to a hollow tunnel. Its walls were made of millions of swirly sparks, linked together like chain mail.

'Follow me, Paige,' Storm barked, leaping into the tunnel-tube.

'Wait for me!' Paige called a second later, dashing after him.

The magic tunnel was springy underfoot and the walls rippled, bouncing Paige along, so that in no time at all she suddenly shot out with a loud *Pop!* Storm sat on the pavement, waiting for her.

'Oh! That was fantastic!' Paige gasped, swaying slightly. Her legs felt quite wobbly — just like she'd been on a bouncy castle!

She looked around and saw that she and Storm were now in a quiet alleyway behind some wheelie bins. Paige realized where they were. There was a big shopping centre just round the corner.

'Now you can buy Amy a present,'

Storm woofed, looking pleased with himself.

Paige quickly bent down to stroke him. 'Thanks, Storm.'

She didn't waste any time, as they had to get back before Debs returned and noticed they were both gone. Paige hurried into a big store and went straight to the toy department. Amy was mad about fairies and had heaps of fairy books. She even had a string of fairy lights around her wall mirror.

Paige chose a fairy dolly with a lavender dress and crown and matching glittery wings. 'Perfect! Isn't she pretty?' she whispered to Storm. 'Have I got time to get a card?'

'Yes, but you will have to hurry. This

sort of magic does not last long,' Storm barked softly.

Paige set off again, but on reaching the card department she stared in dismay. 'There're about a hundred million cards here. I don't know which one to choose.'

Storm waved one tiny front paw and a shower of golden glitter shot out. From out of the corner of her eye, Paige noticed a fairy-shaped card glowing as brightly as a star on one of the racks. As she picked it up and opened it, tinkling fairy music played 'Happy Birthday'.

'Yay! Amy will love this!' Paige went and paid and then hurried outside into the alleyway after the little puppy.

The golden tube began to fade as

Paige got close. There was no time to waste. She and Storm plunged in and once again, Paige felt the tunnel's springy walls and floor helping them along.

Suddenly, the tube began to ripple much faster than before and Paige and Storm went shooting forward.

'Ooer!' she cried as, with a loud burping noise, the tunnel spat them

both out and they landed on their bottoms on the kitchen floor. The tunnel began to dissolve into fizzing sparks before disappearing with a final loud *Pop!*

Paige gingerly picked herself up and grinned. 'That was so much fun and I've got a brilliant present for Amy. Thank you, Storm!'

The tiny puppy's little muzzle wrinkled in his cute Dalmatian grin. 'I am glad I was able to help.'

Paige had barely caught her breath, when the kitchen door swung open and Debs came in.

'Hello, darling. Discussing all those books has made me hungry. I think it's time for dinner. Have you and Storm been having a good time?' she asked.

'Er . . . yeah!' Paige said, winking at the tiny puppy. *You'd never believe me, even if I told you*, she thought.

On Friday, Debs insisted on booking a taxi, so Paige and Storm arrived in style at Amy's house. Storm was invisible, to save Paige having to offer awkward explanations.

'Happy Birthday!' Paige gave Amy her card and present.

Tori stood by as Amy unwrapped it. 'Oh, I absolutely love her!' Amy said delightedly, clutching her lavender fairy doll. 'How did you know?'

'Know what?' Paige asked, puzzled.

Amy and Tori exchanged knowing glances. 'Come and see!' They practically hauled Paige into the kitchen.

Paige's eyes widened as she saw the
pink tablecloth strewn with sequins,
the plates of dainty food and the big
birthday cake in the shape of a fairy
castle. There were sparkly pink and
violet streamers trailing down the walls.

'It's a *total* fairy party! Don't you just
love it?' Amy said.

'Wow! It looks . . . magical!' Paige
said delightedly.

They played Pin the Wing on the
Fairy. Everyone fell about laughing
when Amy's dad pinned the wing on
the fairy's nose. There was Pass the
Magic Parcel and then a dressing–up
game with cardboard, tinsel and
coloured tissue and a prize for the best
fairy costume. Tori won it easily.

'Wait until you see what we're doing

at *my* party,' Tori said to Paige. 'It's
going to be very grown-up. Fairies
are OK, but they're a bit babyish,
aren't they?' she said, flicking back
her long hair.

'Amy doesn't seem to think so.
Neither do I,' Paige replied. 'Aren't you
having fun?'

'Well – yes,' Tori admitted.

'What are you moaning about then,
you muppet!' Paige joked, giving her a
friendly dig in the ribs.

Tori laughed. 'It's so great that our
birthdays are so close together, isn't it?
We're the Party Girls!' she said, doing
a twirl.

Not this year, Paige thought sadly,
but she didn't want to spoil the happy
mood by saying anything yet.

When no one was watching, Paige gave Storm some party treats. He sat on the window sill, enjoying watching the party without being trodden on. 'I like party food,' he woofed happily, chomping his fairy-sized sandwiches and crisps.

When Paige's taxi arrived to take her home, Amy's mum handed her a pink satin goody bag. Paige said her thank yous and goodbyes and Amy and Tori waved from the doorstep. 'See you at my party on Monday!' Tori called.

Storm sat on Paige's lap in the back of the taxi. 'I don't mind going back to Debs's too much. I'm starting to quite like her,' Paige sighed, stroking his soft spotty fur. 'But it feels mega-wrong not to have a party. Especially as me,

Amy and Tori have spent ages talking about it.'

Storm whined sympathetically.

Debs was waiting eagerly at the door to let Paige and Storm in. 'Tell me everything and don't leave anything out! What did your friends say when they saw Storm? Did you tell them you were looking after a puppy?'

'Um, yes. They made a big fuss of

Storm,' Paige said. She quickly changed the subject. 'Amy's party had a fairy theme. It looked so pretty . . .' she said.

Debs listened as Paige told her about the games and the yummy party food. 'I've been thinking,' she said when Paige had finished. 'It's a shame that you can't celebrate your birthday properly with your mum in hospital. How would you like a tea party here, for you, Amy and Tori?'

'Really?' Paige said, surprised. She hadn't the heart to tell Debs that she'd been looking forward to something a bit more special. A tea party didn't sound all that exciting. 'Thanks very much. That would be . . . very nice.'

Debs beamed. 'That's settled then.'

Chapter
SIX

The next time Keith took Paige and
Storm to the hospital to visit her mum,
she made sure she asked him to take
her shopping afterwards.

'OK then. But I'm in a bit of a rush.
Do you know which shop you need?'
Keith said.

Paige nodded. She knew just what
Tori wanted. She bought her a CD of

her favourite boy band, a pack of coloured gel pens and a card in the shape of a shiny designer handbag. 'And can we just pop back to the flat? I want to get some clothes. I'll be super-quick!' she pleaded.

Keith drove to their block and sat outside with the engine running, while Paige dashed up the stairs and along the concrete walkway. Storm followed Paige into her bedroom and flopped down on her fluffy floor cushion while she burrowed in the wardrobe.

'I like this place,' he woofed, looking around at the bright posters on the walls.

'Me too! It's tiny but it's all mine,' Paige said, stuffing a blue top with a sparkly butterfly and her newest jeans into her bag. It felt comforting being back home among her snow domes, framed pictures and old Barbie dolls. She couldn't resist picking up the battered old teddy who always sat on her bed and giving him a cuddle.

When it was time to go, she had to wrench herself away. She sighed sadly as she shouldered her bag and quickly locked the front door. 'I wish I didn't

have to go back to Debs. I can't wait until mum comes home and we can be a family again,' she said to Storm as they hurried back down to where Keith was waiting.

Only now, it'll be a different kind of family, she thought worriedly. *One with a tiny smelly fussy baby that demands everyone's attention.*

On Monday night, Paige dressed in her sparkly butterfly top and jeans.

'Oh, you do look pretty. Wait a minute, I've got just the thing to go with that outfit,' Debs said.

Paige pulled a face. 'Oh no. She's probably going to bring me one of her flowing velvet jackets,' she whispered to Storm.

'Is that a bad thing?' Storm woofed
softly, looking puzzled.

'Er . . . yes!' Paige said. 'I can hardly
go out looking like a pair of curtains!'

But Debs returned with a pair of neat
clip-on earrings, the same colour blue
as Paige's top. Paige put them on. 'Oh,
I love them! Thanks, Debs. They're
perfect.'

71

Debs looked pleased. 'Would you like me to do your hair? I've got a set of heated rollers somewhere.'

Paige was thinking how to refuse politely, not wanting to push her luck, when Amy and her mum arrived to pick her up.

'Have a good time,' Debs called as Paige walked down the front garden. 'Oh, just a minute. Haven't you forgotten something? Storm!'

Paige froze. Storm was walking invisibly at her ankles. Debs obviously couldn't see him, so she thought Paige had left him behind. Turning round, she ran back towards Debs. 'I left him in my room. He seemed a bit tired,' she said, hoping Debs wouldn't go upstairs to check.

'What was all that about?' Amy asked
as Paige got into the back seat of the
car and sat next to her. 'She said
something about a storm.'

'Um . . . yes. She thought it might
rain later . . .' Paige said vaguely.
'Anyway, don't let's worry about that.
We've got Tori's brother Dean to worry
about instead. Yuk! I hope he isn't at
the party – he's a real pain.'

'You can say that again,' Amy said.

'He's a real pain,' Paige repeated and
they both laughed.

When they arrived at Tori's house,
Paige spotted a tall thin boy with dark
hair and a pimply face. 'Oh great.
There's Dean,' she whispered to Storm.
'Look out for him. He can be a real
nuisance with his nasty jokes.'

Storm showed his teeth in a tiny growl. 'That is not a good way to act.'

Amy, Paige and Storm wandered into the bright shiny kitchen and gave Tori her presents. There was a big display of expensive gifts on a sideboard. 'Those are all mine. Aren't I lucky?' Tori said proudly.

'Well, you are our bestest sweetest big girl,' her mum cooed, giving her a hug.

Dean pretended to stick his finger in his mouth and made gagging movements. For once, Paige didn't blame him. But then he spoiled it by hanging around and making stupid comments while Tori opened her presents. 'Felt tips! Bor-ring. You're ten, not six, aren't you?' he hooted, when she opened Paige's.

Paige blushed hotly, as she felt Storm nudge her leg protectively with his wet little nose.

Tori just giggled. 'They're gel pens actually. Just what I wanted. And this CD is great. Thanks, Paige.'

'That's OK,' Paige said, glaring at Dean and wishing he'd clear off.

Dean pulled a face at her and sloped out of the kitchen.

'This way, everyone!' Tori cried, leading the way into the sitting room.

The two enormous leather sofas had been pushed back and a shiny covering placed over the carpet to make a dance floor. A stack of disco equipment with big speakers stood near a row of lights flashing different colours.

Paige and Amy were seriously

impressed. 'Wow! It's just like a proper club!' Amy said.

Tori smiled proudly. 'I *told* you I was having a grown-up party. I'll put the CD Paige bought on my new player and we can do our routine to it.'

Paige felt self-conscious with everyone watching. But she soon relaxed and remembered all the steps. Everyone clapped when they finished.

Storm barked excitedly too, but only Paige could hear him. She winked at him when no one was looking.

The dancing was great fun, until Dean joined in. He jumped about, knocking into people on purpose.

'Ow!' Paige cried, when he leapt on her foot. 'Now who's acting like a six-year-old!' she muttered crossly.

Dean's face darkened as he heard her. 'Listen, everyone! Paige's in a rage! I'm really scared,' he mocked.

'You're so pathetic,' Paige said disgustedly, turning her back.

Tori's dad made fruit-juice cocktails with coloured ice cubes and little umbrellas. He handed them round on a tray, like a real waiter. 'Food's ready, when you've finished dancing,' he announced.

Storm followed Paige outside to the super-sized barbecue. His little black nose twitched at the delicious smells wafting towards him. 'That human food smells good,' he woofed.

Paige smiled at him. 'Knowing Tori's parents, there'll be millions of posh sausages and top-notch burgers. You'll love them.'

Everyone trooped over to the tables and chairs on the lawn. Storm sat under Paige's table. She slipped him some meat, but he found plenty to chomp up from all the bits the others dropped. It was all Paige could do not to giggle. He was better than a vacuum cleaner!

'My party's the best in the whole world, isn't it? Wait until you see my cake. It's got three layers *and* sugar roses.

The bottom's chocolate, the middle's lemon and the top's strawberry. It's mega-lush,' Tori said.

Paige fought down a stab of anxiety. Debs's tea party idea was looking more pale and pathetic by the moment. Maybe she should just tell Debs that she didn't want a party after all. Amy and Tori were going to be so disappointed with a dull old tea party.

Paige shook her head sadly as Tori's mum lit the candles on the amazing birthday cake and everyone sang 'Happy Birthday'. Paige took a plate when the multi-coloured slices were handed round, but she didn't feel very hungry any more.

Soon afterwards, parents began arriving to pick up their kids.

'Mum will be here for us soon. I'm going to get my coat,' Amy said.

'OK,' Paige replied. She decided that she'd better fetch Storm. The last time she'd seen him he was exploring the bottom of the garden.

But Paige couldn't find him. He definitely wasn't nosing about in any of the flower beds. Suddenly, a loud yelp of fear came from the direction of the tree house.

Paige gasped as she caught sight of the tiny spotted puppy wobbling on a branch, high above the ground!

Chapter
SEVEN

Paige's pulse raced as she ran towards the tree.

'Come back here, you stupid mutt!' a voice called angrily and Paige saw Dean leaning out of the tree-house window, reaching for the trembling puppy.

Paige realized that Storm must be so scared that he'd forgotten to make himself invisible. He couldn't use his magic to help himself now that Dean could see him.

'Hang on, Storm!' Paige cried as she leapt forward. Suddenly, Storm's paws slipped and his back legs swung in mid-air. His tiny legs scrabbled for a foothold and then he whimpered as he felt himself falling.

Paige's heart missed a beat. She

stretched out her arms and just
managed to catch Storm, but she was
still rushing forward. With the tiny
puppy in her arms, she couldn't put out
her hands to stop herself and crashed
into the tree trunk with a massive *thud*.

Paige fell to the ground, dazed.

'Oh, flipping heck!' Dean cried. He
ducked inside the tree house and began
climbing down.

Paige felt a familiar prickling
sensation down her spine as bright gold
sparks bloomed in Storm's spotty fur
and his little black nose glowed like a
gold nugget. Storm leaned close and
very gently touched her chin with the
tip of his wet nose.

A warm fizzing feeling spread
outwards from Paige's chin. It washed

over her face and forehead and then trickled down over the back of her neck. In just a second she felt as clear-headed as if she'd just eaten a very strong peppermint.

She sat up with Storm still in her lap. Dean appeared beside them, just as every last spark faded from Storm's coat.

'You're sitting up! I thought you —' he said in a panicky voice.

'We're fine. No thanks to you!' Paige fumed, losing her temper. 'What sort of person tries to scare a tiny puppy, especially high up in a tree!'

'I didn't mean to scare him!' Dean snapped, flushing. 'I was just mucking around.' His eyes narrowed. 'How come you know its name, anyway? Is it yours? I didn't see you with it at the party.'

Paige hesitated. 'I've . . . um . . . seen Storm around here before. He must live with one of your neighbours.'

'Funny. I've never seen him,' Dean said suspiciously. 'I'll come with you to take him back.'

'No! I mean, I can do it by myself,' Paige insisted, but her heart sank as she saw the determined look on Dean's face.

As Dean took a step towards Paige, Storm lifted his lip and growled softly. He leapt out of her lap and ran behind the tree.

Paige felt another faint tingling sensation down her spine. A little spurt of gold sparks puffed up from a nearby pile of grass cuttings and vegetable peelings. Suddenly, there was a strong

gust of breeze, which blew the entire
heap towards Dean.

Whoosh! A cascade of compost swept
him off his feet. *Splop!* It covered Dean
up to his neck and held him firmly to
the ground. 'Help!' he croaked, spitting
out shreds of brownish leaves.

Paige left him there. 'You'd better stay
invisible now. Come on, Amy's mum's
probably here to pick us up,' she

whispered to Storm as they hurried back towards the house. 'What you did to Dean was a bit naughty,' she scolded gently. 'But he deserved it!'

Storm's bright blue eyes glowed with mischief. He wrinkled his muzzle in a cute Dalmatian grin. 'Perhaps it will teach that mean boy a lesson. My magic will wear off in a few minutes.'

Paige laughed. 'I'd give two weeks' pocket money to see him trying to explain how a compost heap attacked him! Brothers definitely seem like a real pain.'

Storm put his head on one side. 'But having a baby brother might be different. He would be little and helpless and it would be someone to look after,' he woofed softly.

'Maybe,' Paige said, not convinced.

She felt a surge of affection for the tiny puppy. She knew that Storm meant well and didn't want to hurt his feelings by disagreeing. But she was still very far from being happy about having to share her mum with the baby.

A couple of evenings later, Paige and Debs sat on the dark blue velvet sofa with Storm curled up between them. They were watching a late-night TV film about some kids who got trapped in a haunted house.

'I'm not sure your mum would approve. Maybe we should switch channels before this film gives you nightmares,' Debs said, reaching for the remote.

'Oh, I watch much worse stuff than this,' Paige fibbed. She felt very grown up, staying up late and eating popcorn with Debs. Besides, nothing could scare her while she was cuddled up in bed with Storm!

She reached down to stroke his smooth warm little body. On the TV, a door in the haunted house creaked open, revealing a four-poster bed and heavy furniture. Storm pricked up his ears and sat straight.

'Groof!' he barked, pawing Paige's arm excitedly. 'Why is your bedroom in that box with moving pictures?'

Paige grinned. It did look just like her bedroom. She'd always thought this house was the perfect setting for a creepy film!

A brilliant idea for a birthday party
jumped into her mind. She was dying
to tell Storm about it now, but she
daren't risk it with Debs sitting so
close.

As soon as the film finished, Paige
jumped up and went into the kitchen
to make Debs a cup of tea. She piled
some biscuits on to a plate and brought
them back in with the tea. She saw that

Storm wasn't on the sofa and decided to go and look for him after she'd spoken to Debs.

'Ooh, lovely. Thanks,' Debs said, taking a sip of tea. 'What have I done to deserve this? Are you after something, young lady?' she joked.

Paige felt herself blushing. 'Well . . . actually, I did want to talk to you about my . . . um . . . birthday tea party,' she said sheepishly.

Debs dunked a ginger nut. 'Fire away then. I'm all ears.'

'I was wondering if Tori and Amy could stay the night. Instead of a tea party, maybe we could have a midnight feast. We could easily all sleep in my bed. I thought we could read ghost stories and play creepy games. It could be a scary sleepover. What do you think?' she asked.

Debs nodded thoughtfully and beamed at Paige. 'You clever old thing, you! I wish I'd thought of it. It's a great idea. I've got some old Halloween decorations in the attic and we could put some candles in glass jam jars. I'll dress up and be your spooky waitress, if you like. How about if I made dead man's hands, skeleton biscuits and blood tablets for the midnight feast?' she said, getting into the swing of things.

'Ooh, yes! That would be fantastic!' Paige cried delightedly. 'Can I help make them?'

'Course you can. That's half the fun. There's a bus into town tomorrow. We can go shopping, if you like. I was going to ask if you wanted to come with me and choose a present. And we could pop and visit your mum if we've got time. What do you think?'

'Yay! Thanks, Debs. You're the best!' Paige threw her arms round Debs and hugged her. She couldn't wait to find Storm and tell him her exciting news.

Chapter
EIGHT

Paige skipped upstairs, expecting to see
the tiny puppy curled up on her bed,
but he was nowhere in sight. 'Storm?'
she said, looking around the room.

She checked under the pillows and
covers and then looked under the bed
and in the wardrobe. But there was still
no sign of Storm. Paige finally found
him underneath the old-fashioned

dressing table, curled into a tight ball against the wall.

'Oh, I get it. We're playing hide-and-seek —' Paige began and then her face changed as she saw that the tiny puppy was trembling. 'What's wrong? Are you sick?'

Storm shook his head, his midnight-blue eyes troubled. 'I sensed that Shadow was close and I heard dogs growling in the street outside the house. I think he has set them on to me,' he whimpered.

Paige felt a stir of alarm, but she hadn't heard anything with the TV on. She went and peered through a crack in the curtains, but the street below was empty. 'There aren't any dogs there now,' she told him. 'How will I know they're Shadow's dogs if they come back?'

Storm lifted his head. 'They will be ordinary dogs, with fierce pale eyes and extra-long sharp teeth. Shadow's magic will make any dog I meet into my enemy now.'

'Then we'll have to make sure that you keep well hidden,' Paige said. She managed to reach right underneath the dressing table with one hand and stroke Storm reassuringly.

The terrified puppy slowly uncurled

and finally crept out with his belly
brushing against the carpet. Paige
picked him up and gently tucked him
into bed. 'There, you're safe now. I hope
that horrible Shadow will keep right on
going and fall into the sea! Then you
can stay with me forever and live in
our flat,' she said.

Storm peeped over the covers, his
little face serious. 'I cannot do that.
One day I must return to my own
world and the Moon-claw pack. Do
you understand that, Paige?' he
woofed.

Paige nodded sadly but she didn't
want to think about that now. She
loved having Storm all to herself.
Climbing on to the bed, she curled
herself round Storm.

'I've just been talking to Debs. I've got some great news about my party . . .'

Paige grinned at the squeals of delight coming down the phone the following day when she told Amy and Tori about her party. They were both at Tori's house listening to CDs.

'A scary sleepover is so cool!' Amy said.

'Yes. Almost as good as my party,' Tori said.

'See you both on Saturday! And remember to bring your PJs.' Paige replaced the phone before turning to Storm. 'I'm going into town with Debs now. I'd love you to come with us, but I'm worried about Shadow finding you.'

'I am too,' Storm barked, his bright eyes flickering with fear. 'You go with Debs and I will stay here and hide.'

'OK then, if you're sure. See you later. We'll bring you a treat back,' Paige promised.

Although she had a lovely day with Debs in town, she couldn't help feeling anxious. What if Storm's enemies came back? He might have to leave without even saying goodbye. The thought of Storm leaving made her realize how much she adored her magical friend. She felt determined to enjoy every precious moment with him.

'Would you like something to wear for your birthday?' Debs asked. They were on the way back to the bus stop

with bulging carrier bags and had stopped outside a clothes shop.

'OK,' Paige said, hiding her impatience for Debs's sake. Inside the shop, she dashed up to the first rack and grabbed a black–and–silver top in her size. 'Can I have this, please?'

Debs raised her eyebrows. 'Don't you want to try it on?'

'No. This size fits me fine. I love it. It's just right for my sleepover.'

'All right. If you're sure,' Debs said. She paid for the top and they set off for the bus.

It was only half an hour later, but to Paige it felt like hours before the bus dropped them at the bottom of the lane in Brookton. The moment they got in the house, she dumped her carrier bag in the kitchen and shot upstairs.

'I need the loo!' she shouted over her shoulder at a surprised Debs.

As soon as she went into the bedroom, Paige saw Storm's little spotty tail sticking out from under one of the pillows. 'I'm back. Storm!' she crooned happily, gently uncovering him. She picked him up and cuddled him, breathing in his clean puppy smell. 'I'm so glad that you're still here! My scary sleepover party wouldn't be any fun without you.'

'I am looking forward to that very much,' Storm yapped, his pink tongue darting out as he covered her chin and nose in warm little licks.

'Happy Birthday, love!' Mrs Riley said, handing Paige her card and presents.

As Paige opened them, her face lit up. She had some new trainers, a Hunt the Monster board game and a gift card for downloading music. 'Wow! Thanks. These are brilliant!' she said, hugging her mum and then Keith.

Storm sat beneath the visitor's chair. As there'd been no more sign of any

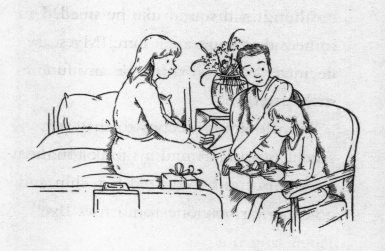

enemy dogs, he and Paige had decided
that it was safe for him to come too.

At the end of visiting time, Paige
kissed her mum. Paige thought she
looked a bit pale. 'Are you OK?' she
asked her.

'Yes, fine. Your brother's a bit restless,
that's all.'

Paige remembered what Storm had
said to her about having a new little

brother. It did sound like he needed someone to look after him. Paige decided that she'd think about it some more later on.

'Have a lovely sleepover party, pet. And I wouldn't mind a slice of birthday cake!' her mum said.

'I'll bring you one tomorrow. Bye!' Paige sang out.

Chapter
NINE

Paige and Debs worked flat out, getting things ready for the party. Paige helped decorate gingerbread men biscuits with black-and-white icing for skeletons. The blood tablets turned out to be tiny strawberry-jam sandwiches. But the dead man's hands were her favourites.

'These are dead clever. Dead, get it!'

Paige joked, filling clear plastic food gloves with popcorn, before tying the ends and dipping the finger tips into pink icing.

Debs laughed. 'That's a truly terrible joke.'

Paige smiled at Storm, who was 'helping' by crunching up any bits of popcorn that escaped. Time seemed to fly and Paige had to run upstairs to get changed.

She had just thrown on her new black-and-silver top, when the doorbell rang. Paige came downstairs, with Storm at her heels to let her friends in.

Amy beamed at Storm as he wagged his tail in a friendly fashion. 'Oh, what a cute puppy! Is he yours?' she said, fussing over him.

Tori bent down to stroke Storm too. 'Was he a present for your birthday? You never said you were getting a puppy. What's he called?'

'Storm,' Paige said. 'He's . . . er . . . not mine. I'm just looking after him for someone while I'm staying here. Debs has been great about it.'

'Did someone mention my name?' called a deep hollow voice. Debs glided into the hall, wearing flowing black clothes. Her face was milk white and her mouth was a slash of red. 'I am Paige's witchy godmother and I am at your service for tonight! This way, please!'

Paige was impressed. Debs was very convincing. She must have been a really good actress.

Amy and Tori's eyes widened in delight when they saw the party food. The dead man's hands were a huge success. The birthday cake was an extra surprise from Debs. It was shaped into a monster face, with sugared jelly-worm hair, a liquorice nose and eyebrows and gobstopper eyeballs.

Debs made a magic potion by

scooping ice cream into glasses of cola
before handing them round.

Paige loved her presents. Amy's was a
comedy DVD called *Revenge of the
Monster Moles*. Tori had bought her an
expensive-looking notebook and
matching folder and some sparkly hair
slides.

'Your chamber is ready, young ladies,
if you'd like to follow me upstairs,' Debs
said in her spooky voice.

'I can't wait to see their faces when
they see my room,' Paige whispered to
Storm.

Plastic bats and spiders hung from the
ceiling. Red-and-black streamers and
fake spiders' webs decorated the bed,
and candles glowed from inside jam
jars on the window sill.

'I can*not* believe that bed!' Tori jumped on to it and lay spread out like a starfish. 'Come on. Let's get our PJs on!'

They all undressed and got into bed. Even with three girls and a puppy in the bed, there was still heaps of room. Storm curled up on the pillow next to Paige. Tori and Amy made a huge fuss of him.

'I wish I had a puppy like yours,' Tori crooned. 'I'm going to make my mum and dad buy me one exactly like Storm,' she decided.

Paige bit back a grin. 'I think they'd have a job. Storm's one of a kind,' she said, smiling fondly at him.

Tori looked a teeny bit put out. 'He's not the only Dalmatian puppy in the world, you know,' she said huffily.

'You're so lucky, Paige,' Amy said. 'Debs is great and you can stay in this amazing house whenever you like. And you're going to have a sweet little baby brother soon.'

'I wish I had a young brother or sister. I'd love to cuddle a baby and take it for walks in its pram,' Tori sighed.

Paige hadn't considered it like that. Maybe Amy and Tori were right. She'd thought her friends were the lucky ones and now it seemed like they envied her.

Tori suddenly grinned. 'Anyway,' she said, changing the subject. 'I thought this was supposed to be a scary sleepover. I've not exactly been scared of anything yet.'

Paige saw Storm dive under the

bedclothes and then felt a familiar prickling sensation. What was he up to?

'Whoooo! Whoooo!' A loud noise wailed suddenly. All the spiders, bats and ghost shapes leapt off the walls and zoomed towards the end of the bed, where they hovered in the air before shooting back into place.

'Argh!' Tori screamed delightedly. 'That was brilliant. How did you do it?'

'Sound effects and . . . er . . . hidden wires,' Paige said, winking at Storm as he reappeared and snuggled up next to her.

'I nearly wet myself with fright!' Amy exclaimed. 'This is the best party ever.'

'Until mine, next year . . . what?' Tori said as Paige and Amy grabbed a pillow each and battered her.

They made a pact to stay up all night, but after playing Paige's Hunt the Monster game and giggling for an hour as they swapped silly jokes, they snuggled down together. Amy and Tori went to sleep first.

'Goodnight, Storm,' Paige whispered, her eyelids drooping.

'Goodnight, Paige,' Storm woofed, sighing contentedly.

Paige's eyes snapped open. A noise somewhere outside the house had woken her. She reached for Storm, but there was only a tiny warm place next to her where the puppy had been.

Paige crept quietly out of bed, so that she didn't wake Tori and Amy, and tiptoed out on to the dark landing.

From the window, she could see two
fierce dogs sniffing about in the front
garden. Moonlight glinted on their pale
eyes and extra-sharp teeth.

Paige gasped. Shadow's dogs! Storm
was in terrible danger. The moment she
had been dreading was here. Her heart
pounded as she knew she was going to
have to be strong for Storm's sake.

Suddenly, a bright flash of gold light
streamed out from the open bathroom

door at the far end of the landing.
Paige threw herself forward and rushed
inside.

Storm stood there, a tiny spotty
puppy no longer, but a majestic
young silver-grey wolf with a
glittering neck-ruff. An older she-wolf
with a gentle face stood next to him.

Tears pricked Paige's eyes. 'Your
enemies are here! Save yourself, Storm!'
she burst out.

Storm's big midnight-blue eyes
narrowed with affection. 'You have been
a true friend, Paige. Be of good heart,'
he said in a velvety growl.

'I'll never forget you, Storm,' Paige
said, her voice catching.

There was a final dazzling flash and
big gold sparks filled the bathroom and

floated down around Paige and crackled as they hit the floor. Storm and his mother faded and then were gone.

A furious snarling sounded outside in the front garden, but then all was silent.

Paige stood there, still stunned by how fast it had all happened. Her heart ached, but she was glad that she'd had a chance to say goodbye to her magical friend. She knew that she would always remember the time she'd spent with him.

She looked up with tears in her eyes to see Debs standing there. 'Paige? Did the telephone wake you? Keith's just phoned. You've got a beautiful baby brother. He was born a few minutes ago. Apparently he's got the most amazing dark-blue eyes.'

Just like Storm, Paige thought, with a

sense of wonder. She had a sudden thought. 'What time is it?' she asked.

'About ten minutes to midnight,' Debs told her.

Her little brother had been born on her birthday! She was a big sister now. Paige felt an unexpected warmth flood through her at the thought of meeting her tiny helpless brand-new little brother. Wherever he was, she knew that Storm was smiling in approval.

Magic Puppy

A Forest Charm

Prologue

The young silver-grey wolf padded through the trees. Patches of snow still lay on the hillside, gleaming in the spring sunlight. Storm lifted his head. It felt good to breathe the cold air of his home.

Suddenly, a terrifying howl rang out.

'Shadow!' Storm gasped. The fierce lone wolf who had attacked the

Moon-claw pack and wounded Storm's mother was very close.

There was a flash of bright golden light and a shower of dazzling sparks. Where the young wolf had been standing there now crouched a tiny puppy with fluffy white fur, a stocky body and short legs.

Storm whined with terror and his little puppy heart beat fast. He hoped this disguise would protect him from his enemy.

His puppy paws kicked up the soft snow as he tore through the trees. There was a steep ridge ahead of him. Perhaps there would be somewhere to hide. Storm glimpsed a tangle of tree roots that had formed a natural cave and headed towards them.

As he approached, Storm saw wolf eyes gleaming from within the darkness of the roots. He caught his breath and skidded to a halt, ready to turn and run away as fast as he could.

'Storm! In here, quickly!' the wolf called out in a soft growl.

'Mother,' Storm sighed with relief. He rushed forward and pushed through the tangled roots until he reached the she-wolf.

'It is good to see you again, my son,' Canista rumbled, licking her disguised cub's fluffy white fur and little square muzzle.

Storm yipped a greeting. He wriggled his body and wagged his stumpy tail as he licked his mother's face. 'I have come back to lead the Moon-claw pack!'

Canista's gentle eyes lit up with pride. 'Bravely said, but now is not the time. Shadow wants to be leader and he is too strong for you. He has already killed your father and litter brothers and left me weak from his poisoned bite.'

Storm curled his lip in a growl, showing small sharp teeth. He knew that his mother was right, but he was reluctant to leave her.

'The other wolves will not follow Shadow – they are waiting for you. Go back to the other world. Use this disguise. Return when you are stronger and wiser, and then face Shadow.' As Canista finished speaking, she gave a wince of pain.

Storm huffed out a shimmering gold puppy breath, which swirled around his

4

mother's wounded paw and then disappeared into her grey fur.

Canista narrowed her eyes. 'Thank you. The pain is easing.'

Another fierce howl rang out, sounding much closer.

'Shadow knows you are here. Go. Save yourself!' Canista urged.

Bright gold sparks bloomed in the tiny puppy's downy white fur. Storm whimpered as he felt the power building inside him. The gold light around him grew brighter. And brighter . . .

Chapter
ONE

Cassie Yorke stamped moodily through the forest in her new walking boots. She was with her mum and dad and about twenty other adults and kids.

'Why do we have to do this stupid family team-building thing anyway?' she complained.

Mrs Yorke gave her daughter a patient smile. 'That's the third time you've asked me that since leaving home, Cassie. Your dad's new boss is really keen on encouraging his staff to get along well with each other. And that includes their families. This weekend is a way of us working as a team and getting to know each other better,' she explained.

'But we're going to be camping. How

can that be a challenge?' Cassie asked.

'Ever tried camping without a tent to sleep in, a stove to cook on and no water on tap?' her dad asked.

'No way!' Cassie said, horrified.

Her mum laughed. 'We are meant to have fun too. Now try and lose the long face, Cass. OK?'

Cassie sighed heavily and felt her shoulders drooping to match her face. Traipsing through a cold muddy forest on a Friday afternoon was definitely *not* her idea of fun! She had been planning to curl up by the log fire in the sitting room and finish reading her book. *Lost in the Amazon* was the latest in the series about the amazing adventures of ace explorer Jilly Atkins.

Her dad came over and put his arm

round her shoulder. 'Come on, Cass. Where's your spirit of adventure? Just try and imagine you're Jilly Atkins!' he suggested cheerily.

'As if!' Cassie said.

Jilly was tall, strong and brave and fearless. Not small and rather dumpy, like Cassie felt, and she had probably never been teased for being a slowcoach when doing school sports.

'Here we are now,' Mrs Yorke said as the group came in sight of a large wooden cabin with a sign above the door that read *Wild Wood Experiences*.

After the welcome and introductions, two instructors divided the group into teams: the Reds, Blues and Greens. Cassie and her mum and dad were in the Reds.

'Oh great. We've been teamed up
with Ronson from the office. He's a
real know-it-all,' Mr Yorke said softly.

Cassie saw a fit-looking man who
towered over her dad. Mr Ronson was
tanned and broad-shouldered and

looked as if he practically lived at the gym. His wife and daughter were both slim and dark-haired.

'Well, we're supposed to be getting to know each other better. Shall we go over and say hello?' Cassie said.

Mr Yorke gave her a mournful look. Despite herself, Cassie couldn't help smiling.

As the adults exchanged greetings, Cassie went over to Mr Ronson's daughter. 'Hi, I'm Cassie.'

'I'm Erin,' the girl said, tossing her long silky hair over her shoulder.

Cassie looked at her enviously. She wished her hair would grow that long, but her blonde curls just seemed to grow outwards and get bushier.

Erin didn't really say much. Cassie

thought she might be shy, so she made a special attempt to be friendly. 'I'm dreading this. I've never been even normal camping or anything. Have you?' she asked, smiling.

Erin shrugged. 'No, but I've done loads of outdoor stuff with my dad. This is going to be easy-peasy. But how come *you're* here? The rules say you have to be at least ten before you can take part.'

'I'm almost eleven actually,' Cassie said, her smile wavering.

'But you're so small! I thought you were only about eight,' Erin said rudely, looking Cassie up and down.

'My gran says good things always come in small packages,' Cassie shot back. She was used to people making comments about her size and usually found that making a joke of it got over any awkwardness.

But Erin didn't even grin. 'Yeah, well, your gran would have to say that, wouldn't she? I just hope you're not going to hold our team back. My dad only plays to win. He always says that you don't get any prizes for coming second.'

Good for him, Cassie thought, starting to feel rattled. 'My dad's motto is "It's the taking part that counts". I like that one much better!'

'Huh!' Erin gave Cassie a pitying look before flouncing over to stand with her mum.

Mrs Yorke noticed her daughter's annoyed face. 'Are you OK, Cassie? You're not still sulking, are you?'

'Of course not. I'm fine now,' Cassie fibbed, pasting on her best fake smile.

After meeting Erin, Cassie wished more than ever that she could be at home with her head in her book. There didn't seem much chance of the two of them making friends this weekend.

Before the teams set off into the forest, the instructors gathered them all together again for a few words about health and safety. Cassie's tummy suddenly growled, making everyone laugh.

It had been a long drive to get there and lunch seemed like hours ago. Cassie felt more than ready for a snack. There were some crisps and chocolate in her rucksack, but she hesitated about getting them out. Erin was looking her way and she didn't fancy getting any more sarcastic comments.

As people stood about chatting outside the cabin, Cassie saw a chance to slip away. 'Just popping to the loo!' she called to her dad.

'OK, honey. Don't be long,' he said.

Cassie headed past the loo and nipped

smartly round the back of the cabin. She was alone with just the open forest in front of her. Fishing in her rucksack, she drew out a bar of chocolate.

'Yum, yum,' Cassie breathed, licking her lips.

She was about to take a big luxurious bite, when suddenly, a dazzling bright flash of gold light shot out in all directions from the bush in front of her.

Cassie blinked hard, blinded for a moment. She rubbed her eyes and saw a tiny cute puppy with fuzzy white fur, a stocky body and short legs crawling out of the bush.

'Can you help me, please?' it woofed.

Chapter
TWO

Cassie gaped at the little white puppy in utter amazement and the chocolate bar slipped from her numb fingers on to the ground.

She must be so hungry that she was hearing things! Talking puppies didn't just appear to small rather ordinary girls. Even Jilly Atkins had never met one and she'd explored all kinds of strange and remote places.

Cassie shook her head, laughing at herself. Her dad always said that she had an over-active imagination.

'Hello, you,' she crooned, rubbing her fingers together to encourage the tiny puppy to come closer. 'I think you must be a little Westie. Aren't you gorgeous? I wonder which of the instructors you belong to.'

The puppy pricked its ears, and two bright midnight-blue eyes looked up at her from behind a little fringe of fluffy white fur. 'I belong to no one but myself. I am Storm of the Moon-claw pack.'

Cassie did a double take. She snatched her hand back as if it had been burned. 'Y-you really c-can talk?' she gasped.

'Yes, I can. Who are you?' the puppy yapped.

Cassie still couldn't quite believe this was happening, but she didn't want to scare the amazing puppy away. She squatted down to make herself seem smaller and less threatening.

The puppy pricked its ears and put its little head on one side, waiting for her to answer. Although Storm was really

tiny, he seemed quite sure of himself.

'I'm Cassie. Cassie Yorke. I'm here with my parents to do some family team building. It's part of Dad's new job,' she explained.

Storm bent his neck in a formal bow. 'I am honoured to meet you, Cassie.' He took a few steps closer and reached out his neck.

Cassie grinned delightedly as the cute puppy's button-like black nose twitched and then she felt the little wet tip brushing against her fingers. She gently rubbed Storm's soft chest and then moved up to stroke his ears.

It still felt really weird to be having a conversation with a puppy, but Cassie's curiosity began to take over from her initial shock. 'We're miles from anywhere in the middle of this forest. How come you're here if you don't belong to anyone?' she asked, puzzled.

Storm's tiny body began trembling all over like a leaf. 'An evil lone wolf called Shadow is looking for me. He killed my father and litter brothers and injured my mother. Shadow wants to lead the Moon-claw pack, but the others will not follow him while I live.'

'But you're just a helpless little puppy. Why would an evil wolf –' Cassie began.

Storm backed away. 'I will show you!'

There was another flash of bright gold light, and big sparks rained down all around Cassie and sizzled on the damp forest floor as they landed.

'Oh!' Cassie cried, blinking hard. But

as her sight cleared, she caught her breath.

The tiny white puppy had disappeared and in its place there crouched a majestic young silver-grey wolf with bright midnight-blue eyes. Specks of gold dust gleamed in its fur and shone from within its deep neck-ruff.

Cassie eyed the wolf's sharp teeth and

powerful muscles. 'Storm?' she breathed nervously.

'Yes, it is me. Do not be afraid. I will not harm you,' Storm told her in a deep velvety growl.

While Cassie was still struggling to take in the sight of Storm as his magnificent real self, there was a final dazzling flash and Storm reappeared once more as a tiny white scared-looking West Highland terrier puppy.

'Wow! That's an amazing disguise!' Cassie said, completely overwhelmed by what had just happened. 'Shadow will never recognize you now.'

Storm blinked up at Cassie with a troubled expression. 'Shadow will use his magic to find me as soon as he can and then no disguise will protect me. I need to hide now. Can you help me?'

Cassie's soft heart went out to the terrified little puppy. With his bright blue eyes peeking out from behind a downy fringe, his square little face and pricked ears, he was the most adorable thing she had ever seen. 'I'd really love to. But I don't see how I can,' she said, chewing her lip. 'We have to take part in lots of horrible exercises. I bet some of the families might think a puppy would slow us down too much.' Cassie frowned as she thought about the Ronsons in particular.

'Do not worry, Cassie!' Storm barked softly, jumping up and pawing her waterproof trousers. 'I will use my magic so that only you can see and hear me!'

'You mean – you can make yourself invisible? Cool! Then you can come with me. Maybe you should do it now before someone sees you.'

Storm shook himself, so that tiny

sparks flew out of his fluffy white fur. 'It is done.'

'Yay! It's going to be brilliant having someone nice I can talk to this weekend,' Cassie said. 'Wait until I tell Dad about you. He's great at keeping secrets!'

'No! Only you must know I am here. You can never tell anyone. Promise me, Cassie,' Storm woofed, his little face serious.

Cassie felt disappointed that she couldn't even tell her dad the exciting news. But Storm looked so scared, gazing up at her with pleading blue eyes. Cassie decided then and there that if it would help to keep Storm safe, she was prepared to agree.

'OK. Cross my heart and chips don't

fly! That's my own way of saying I promise,' she said as Storm's furry white brow wrinkled in a puzzled frown.

'I've been looking everywhere for you!' an irritated voice suddenly demanded from behind her.

Cassie froze as she recognized Erin's bossy tone.

'Who on earth are you talking to?'

Chapter
THREE

Cassie whipped round guiltily. 'Me? I
was just talking to . . . er . . . myself,'
she said hastily.

'Your dad sent me to find you,' Erin
grumbled. 'I thought you said that you'd
be in the girls' loos.'

'Um . . . yeah. I've just . . . er . . .
finished in there,' Cassie said distractedly.
'I forgot the way back.'

Storm was sitting there large as life
barely a metre away. Even though
Storm had said he was now invisible,
Cassie couldn't quite believe it. She
tensed, waiting for Erin to notice the
little puppy. But the older girl didn't
comment and Cassie began to relax.

'I'm coming now,' she said, reaching
for her rucksack.

'About time too,' Erin scolded.

Storm was now rolling on his back
in the grass. He looked as cute as could
be with his fat pale tummy showing
and all four of his short white legs in
the air. Cassie had to try really hard
not to giggle.

'What's so funny?' Erin asked crossly.

'Nothing,' she said, forcing herself to
concentrate. Luckily, Storm stood up
and shook himself just as an extra big
giggle rose up in her chest. Cassie
hastily turned it into a cough. 'Sorry . . .
er . . . frog in my throat. I bet it's going
to take ages to make a fire and build a
shelter and stuff,' she said, quickly
changing the subject.

Erin smirked. 'Not with *my* dad
helping, it won't! Mum says he's a

whizz with power tools. He can make anything. He made me a brilliant tree house, with a ladder and slide and everything.'

I'd like to see him try to plug in an electric screwdriver in the middle of the forest, Cassie thought, fed up with Erin's boasting.

'Hey!' Erin cried, spotting the chocolate bar on the ground. She swooped down and picked it up. 'Is that yours? You've been having a secret scoff, haven't you?'

'No, I have not!' Cassie said truthfully. Well, it was true that she hadn't eaten any chocolate – yet. And after finding Storm, she'd forgotten all about it. 'Anyway, so what? It's only one measly little bar.'

'It's against the rules to bring your own food. Let's see what the others have to say when I show them this!' Erin waved the bar in the air triumphantly.

'Give it back!' Cassie cried, jumping up to try and reach it, but Erin kept dodging out of her way.

Suddenly, Storm streaked upwards, shedding a glittering rocket's trail of gold sparkles behind him. He shot between Cassie and Erin, grasping the bar in his sharp little teeth. Tossing his head, he pulled the chocolate out of Erin's hand.

'What —' Erin looked up in surprise at her empty hand.

Storm drifted to the ground in another flurry of sparks. Laying back his ears, he bounded away into the bushes.

Cassie bit back another grin. Because Erin couldn't see Storm, she must have thought the chocolate had made a bid to escape by leaping into the air all by itself!

'I don't get it. Where's that chocolate gone?' Erin said, frowning.

'Beats me,' Cassie said casually. She didn't even mind losing the chocolate bar. It was worth it to see the look on Erin's snooty face! Cassie slung her rucksack over her shoulder. 'What are you waiting for? I thought we were in a hurry.'

Still looking puzzled, Erin began following Cassie.

Storm exploded out of the bushes in a flurry of leaves and came tearing over to Cassie with a wide cheeky grin on his little square white face.

'Thanks, Storm. You were brilliant. I don't think Erin will bother snitching on me now that the evidence has gone!' she whispered.

'I am glad I was able to help,' Storm woofed. He stretched and then kicked at the ground with his short back legs, sending a tiny spray of muddy grass in Erin's direction.

Erin skirted sideways to avoid getting spattered. 'There are some mega-freaky breezes in this forest,' she commented.

Cassie thought she was going to burst with laughter. Clapping both hands over her mouth, she broke into a jog. Having Storm as her own special team-mate this weekend was going to be the best fun ever.

Chapter
FOUR

Cassie's spirits were high as the group trekked along a forest track. Storm was gambolling along beside her. Her earlier annoyance at Erin's unfriendliness faded into the background as she thought about her brilliant new puppy friend. The morning flew by and it seemed like about five minutes before they all reached a clearing.

Storm's ears twitched as he looked up at the tall sweet chestnut trees that ringed the area. There were lots of fallen branches, and a thick layer of gold and orange leaves covered everything.

'This is a safe place,' he woofed.

Cassie quickly checked that no one was listening before answering. 'I'm glad you like it. Because it looks like we're

about to set up camp here,' she whispered.

The instructors explained that the Reds, Blues and Greens would need to make everything they needed from materials they could find around them. There would also be a special task for the kids from each team.

'I wonder what that's going to be,' Cassie whispered to Storm.

He sat at Cassie's feet, all attention. His fluffy white bottom was parked on her walking boots. She had to stop herself from bending down to stroke him.

'This suddenly seems like an awful lot of hard work,' her dad said. 'I hope we haven't actually got to hunt for our food as well.' His face was red and sweating from the walk. Cassie could see there were damp patches on his T-shirt through his open shirt.

She gave him a little dig. 'Think of it as a challenge, Dad! The Red team rules, OK!'

He screwed up his face, but then reached across to ruffle her mop of fair curls. 'Well, I'm glad to see that you've perked up. I thought our most difficult task was going to be cheer-up-the-grumpy-daughter!' he teased.

'Da-ad! I wasn't that bad. Was I, Mum?' Cassie said, grinning.

Mrs Yorke smiled and held up her open hands. 'I'm saying nothing!'

Everyone had a drink of bottled water before they started work. Cassie took a swig of hers and then bent down and pretended to be fiddling with her boots. Making sure that no one was watching, she poured some water into her hand for Storm.

His soft whiskery little muzzle tickled her as he lapped it up. 'Thank you, Cassie,' he woofed, licking his chops.

'There'll be a prize for the team who constructs the best shelter and another for the one that gets a fire started first. You might find it helpful to elect a leader,' an instructor was explaining.

Cassie's attention was still on Storm when Mr Ronson's loud voice suddenly made her jump.

'I'll be the Red team's leader,' he boomed. 'I'm the most experienced at outdoor skills. Any objections?' he asked.

'Er . . . well . . .' Mr Yorke murmured, looking a bit stunned.

'No? That's settled then,' Mr Ronson said.

After the Blue and Green teams had decided on their leaders, an instructor explained about the kids' task. 'While the adults build a shelter to sleep in, you're going to look for a hidden parcel, containing fire-making tools. There's one for each team. And there'll be a prize for the team who gets their fire going first.'

'That sounds like fun,' Cassie whispered to Storm. 'And you'll be able to have a good runabout in the forest.'

Storm nodded and eagerly wagged his stumpy tail.

As the teams moved apart and then set to work, Mr Ronson took charge. 'Right. You two can start by collecting some branches. We need to trim them before we use them to build the shelter,' he said, jabbing a finger at Cassie's mum and dad, before turning to his wife. 'And you can collect some twigs for firewood. OK, guys, get to it!' he ordered.

Cassie's dad pulled a wry face at her before he set off towards some fallen branches.

'I see what dad means about Mr Ronson. He's really enjoying bossing everyone about, isn't he? No wonder Erin's so unbearable,' Cassie said to Storm.

Storm growled very softly in agreement.

Cassie suddenly noticed that Erin was looking at her with narrowed eyes and angry flushed cheeks. She realized that she must have spoken more loudly than she'd intended to and Erin had heard her.

She chewed at her lip, feeling guilty. No one liked to hear someone else criticizing their dad. 'Erin, I'm really —'

Cassie was about to apologize, but just then Mr Ronson came over.

'Right, you two. You need to find that hidden package and get back here with it pronto. That prize for lighting a fire first is ours, or I'll want to know the reason why! OK?'

'No problem. I won't let you down, Dad,' Erin said.

'Don't you mean *we* won't let the *team* down?' Cassie asked.

Erin ignored her. 'Does Cassie have to come with me? She'll only lag behind and slow me up!'

Cassie saw Storm's fuzzy white fringe dip in a frown. 'That is not a very kind thing to say!' he yapped.

Cassie agreed with him. 'But I wasn't very nice about her dad, though, was I?

Erin's probably just getting her own back on me,' she whispered to him.

But Storm snorted and didn't seem so sure.

'The task is for both of you. Those are the rules, Erin,' Mr Ronson said. He handed Erin a small map and a piece of chalk. 'Why don't you show Cassie how it's done by setting her a good example?'

'If I have to,' Erin said reluctantly, slanting a sideways look at Cassie. 'But it won't be my fault if she messes up.'

Mr Ronson patted his daughter's arm. He smiled down at Cassie. 'I'm sure you'll do your best, dear. A team's only as strong as its weakest member, you know.'

'Charming,' Cassie fumed quietly, but wisely chose not to say anything.

Erin began studying the map as her
dad walked back to the rest of the Reds.

'Can I have a look?' Cassie asked,
going towards her and peering over her
shoulder.

After they had both worked out the

way to go, Erin crumpled up the map and chucked it on the floor.

'Erin!' Cassie cried, indignant at the older girl's littering. But before she could go and pick the map up, she saw Erin already stomping off through the trees.

'Well, come on then,' Erin called back impatiently.

Cassie sighed and she and Storm set off after her. She decided she would pick the map up on their way back.

At first Erin walked at a normal speed, swinging her arms, but the moment they had left the campsite she broke into a run, tearing away from Cassie and Storm.

'Hey! Hang on!' Cassie called to her, speeding up.

Erin looked over her shoulder and waggled her fingers in a wave. 'Come on then, slowcoach!'

Cassie gritted her teeth in determination and broke into a run. She pumped her arms and legs like pistons as she tried to catch up with long-legged Erin. But it was no use. Erin easily out-paced her and was soon out of sight.

Cassie slowed down and then stopped in frustration. 'Oh fudge! Whopping great slurpy slabs of it. I've always been rubbish at running,' she puffed. 'Erin's just going to get the package by herself and then crow about it to everyone. Maybe she was right about me being useless. I should have stayed behind at the camp.'

'That is not true, Cassie. I will help you to catch her up,' Storm woofed.

Suddenly, Cassie felt a strange tingling sensation flowing down her back as bright gold sparks began igniting in Storm's fluffy white fur, and his pointed white ears crackled with electricity.

Something very strange was about to happen!

Chapter
FIVE

Cassie watched in amazement as Storm
lifted one little white paw and sent a
fountain of gold sparks whooshing
towards her. They swirled around,
whirling faster and faster and then
began forming into the shape of a
magnificent horse with a dazzling white
coat and a flowing gold mane and tail.

The next instant, Cassie found herself

seated on the back of the beautiful horse. 'Wow!' she breathed, patting its warm silky neck. 'This is brilliant!'

Storm leapt up in front of her in another little flurry of sparks and Cassie wrapped her hands in the thick golden mane and held on tight. The horse snorted and pawed the ground with one elegant hoof, before it galloped away in a blur of speed. Storm's fluffy white fur rippled in the breeze as they raced along, searching for Erin.

Cassie laughed with delight as trees flashed past them. Now and then the horse veered expertly to one side to avoid a particularly big tree, or weaved through the tall bracken.

'I feel just like Jilly Atkins in *Outback Trail*,' she told Storm.

'Is Jilly one of your friends?' Storm barked.

'No. She's not a real person. She's a character in books and computer games. But I like her because she's strong and brave and she always tries to do her best.'

Storm turned to look up at her. 'Just like you!'

Cassie smiled at him. No one had ever called her strong and brave before. 'Look, there's Erin!' she cried, pointing at a slim figure standing beneath a spreading oak tree. 'Well done, Storm!'

Once again, Cassie felt a prickling sensation down her spine. There was a flash of golden sparkles. The horse melted into a wisp of white and gold smoke before disappearing with a soft *Pop!* and then she and Storm were standing on the leaf-covered ground behind a thick bush.

Cassie started hurrying towards Erin, with Storm trotting invisibly beside her. She pretended to be out of breath as if she'd been running hard.

Erin turned round as Cassie came

lumbering up to her. 'Oh, it's you,' she said, scowling.

'Thanks very much for waiting for me,' Cassie said sarcastically.

'Well, you should have got a move on. I can't help it if you're a slowcoach,' Erin scoffed.

Cassie felt her temper rise as Erin hit a raw nerve. 'Don't call me that!' she exclaimed in frustration. 'It was your fault I couldn't keep up. You deliberately ran off and left me!'

'OK. Keep your hair on,' Erin said warily, taking a step back. 'Maybe I was a bit too keen to get going. Anyway, you're here now, aren't you? Look. That's where the package must be hidden.' She pointed up into the branches where a red flag was fluttering from a fork in the trunk. 'One of us has to climb up and get it.'

Cassie could see that the flag was fairly high up, but the trunk had plenty of knobbly bits for safe hand and footholds. She paused, expecting Erin to

leap forward and scale the tree in her usual 'me-first' way.

But Erin looked unusually tense. 'Go on then. What are you waiting for? Climb up there, Cassie!'

But Cassie was fed up with being bossed about. 'Why don't we toss for it? Loser climbs up.' She took a ten-pence piece out of her pocket, tossed it and covered the coin with her hand. 'Your call.'

'Heads!' Erin said.

Cassie uncovered the coin. 'It's tails. You lose.'

'How about best of three?' Erin said promptly.

Cassie shrugged. She tossed the coin twice more and won each time. 'Congratulations! You go up the tree.'

The colour drained from Erin's face. She hung her head. 'I . . . er . . . can't,' she murmured.

Cassie frowned. 'Why not? It's a dead easy climb.'

'I don't like heights, OK?' Erin snapped. 'I suppose you think I'm pathetic now, don't you?'

Cassie was shocked. The way Erin had behaved so far, she didn't think the older girl would be afraid of anything. She was tempted to tease Erin now and get her own back, but seeing how nervous Erin looked she decided not to.

'No, I don't think you're pathetic,' Cassie replied. 'It's no big deal. Everyone's scared of something. I'm not that keen on big hairy spiders.'

Erin looked relieved. 'You won't tell

anyone, will you? Dad doesn't believe in being scared of things. He says everyone has to face their fears. That's what he always does.'

'Yeah, well not everybody's that strong,' Cassie said. 'Of course I won't say anything.'

'Thanks,' Erin said, smiling with genuine warmth for the first time since Cassie had met her. She looked much softer and prettier without the scowl she wore so often.

Cassie found herself wondering for the first time whether she and Erin could become friends. It would be really nice as their dads worked together and they'd probably get to meet each other again in the future.

Cassie took a firm handhold on the

oak's trunk and then braced her foot against a ridge of bark. She swung herself up, climbed up to the fork and reached for the package.

From her high vantage point, she smiled as she caught a glimpse of a small white shape diving into some bracken. Storm was obviously chasing a poor rabbit again!

Cassie climbed down carefully. She had barely reached the ground before Erin grabbed the package out of her hands and tore it open. A small key-ring-like object, but with only two small metal tags, fell into her hands.

'The flint and striker. Now we can go back and get a fire started,' Erin said triumphantly. 'I really want to win that prize. Let's go!'

Cassie followed as Erin set off
confidently. But they had only been
walking for a couple of minutes when
Erin stopped and looked around. 'I'm
not sure which way to go now.'

'Me neither. I can't see any chalk
marks on the trees –' Cassie stopped as
she saw the look on Erin's face.

'I forgot to make any,' Erin murmured, looking a bit shame-faced.

And Cassie knew why. Erin had been too intent on leaving her behind to mark a chalk trail back to camp.

Erin's face fell. 'We're completely lost. What are we going to do?'

Chapter
SIX

Cassie knew that Storm would easily be able to follow their scent trail back to camp, but he was busy chasing rabbits. With Erin so close, Cassie couldn't call him. She knew that Storm was bound to come and find her soon, but of course she couldn't tell Erin that.

Cassie tried to think of some way of causing a delay. As she shifted her rucksack, she heard a faint crackling of crisp wrappers.

'I think I'll have a quick snack before we start off again,' she said, playing for time. She sat down and took out a bag of crisps. 'Do you want some?'

Erin looked at her in disbelief. 'No, I don't! Don't you care that we're lost?

How can you just sit there stuffing your face?'

'Dead easily,' Cassie said, munching happily. 'Chill out, Erin. Something will turn up; it always does.'

Erin stamped her feet. 'We're going to be *so* late back. I know my dad's counting on winning both prizes. He'll be furious that he can't start the fire.'

'I thought you said he was an expert at outdoor stuff. Can't he rub two sticks together or something?' Cassie suggested reasonably.

'Don't be stupid. That would take ages!' Erin snapped. 'Right! I'm going to try and find my way back now. You can stay here if you like. See if I care.'

'Will you just hang on for thirty seconds? I'm thinking,' Cassie said.

'Yeah, I can hear the rusty wheels going round,' Erin sneered.

'Ha, ha,' Cassie said, thinking that Erin's new friendliness hadn't lasted very long.

Just then, Storm emerged from some tall bracken. He came dashing over with his tongue lolling out and jumped into Cassie's lap. Bits of twig and leaves speckled his white fur. 'I had a very good time. Are we ready to go back now?' he panted.

Cassie pretended to be doing up her rucksack, so that she could whisper to him. 'Yes, but Erin didn't put chalk marks on the trees, so we don't know which way to go. Can you find the way for us, please?'

Storm jumped on to the ground, his

stumpy tail wagging. 'I will be glad to do that!'

'Great.' Cassie jumped to her feet and dusted herself off. 'I think those crisps must have fed my brain because I can remember the way back now,' she said, winking at Storm. 'Follow me, Erin!'

Erin shook her head slowly as Cassie

stomped off. 'You are so annoying, Cassie Yorke!' she cried.

'That makes two of us then,' Cassie said cheerfully.

As Cassie, Storm and Erin walked back into camp, they saw that all three teams were finishing their lean-to shelters. The Blues and Greens had fires blazing in front of theirs.

Cassie's mum called to her as she approached. 'Everything all right, love?'

'Fine. We found the package,' Cassie replied, smiling.

'Well done,' her mum said warmly.

Mr Ronson frowned at Erin. 'All the other kids got back ages ago. What happened? I expected better from you, Erin.'

Erin hung her head. 'I'm sorry . . . I didn't . . .' she began hesitantly.

Cassie felt sorry for her. It couldn't be much fun having such a strict dad. 'It was my fault. I forgot to put any chalk marks on the trees, so we got lost,' she interrupted quickly. 'Erin was great though. We were wandering about for ages, but she somehow found the way back here.'

Mrs Ronson put her arm round her daughter. 'Did you? Well done, Erin.'

Erin threw Cassie a grateful look and gave her a rather shaky smile as she handed the flint and striker to her dad. 'Well, at least we can get the fire started now. Better late than never, I suppose,' Mr Ronson sighed.

'That was a good thing to do. You

are a kind human, Cassie,' Storm woofed.

'Thanks, Storm. But I think even Erin deserves to be rescued from such a bossy dad!' she whispered to him, smiling.

Cassie and Storm went to see how their lean-to was coming along. It had a square frame made of branches lashed together. More branches leaning against it formed a slanting open-fronted shelter. Inside it, a thick layer of dried leaves made a soft surface for sleeping on.

'It looks quite cosy in there now, doesn't it?' Cassie said.

Storm seemed to agree. He immediately bounded into the shelter and began nosing around. Leaves flew

in all directions as he scuffed them up
with his front paws.

'Careful. Someone might notice all
this stuff being stirred up by itself,'
Cassie gently reminded him.

Storm put his head on one side,
grinning apologetically. 'I am sorry,
Cassie. There are so many interesting
smells here. I am enjoying exploring
and rooting into everything.'

'Well, that's what puppies do, don't
they?' Cassie said fondly.

Storm nodded happily and suddenly
dashed off towards an interesting-looking
tree stump.

Cassie hid a grin as she watched him.
She felt a surge of affection for her cute
mischievous friend.

Later, Cassie secretly shared her meal

of tinned beans and sausages with him. The light began to fade as they were clearing away and the moon rose over the trees. An owl hooted as Cassie was spreading out her sleeping bag.

Erin came over to put hers next to Cassie. 'Thanks for what you said to my dad about it being your fault that we got lost,' she said quietly as they both got ready for bed.

'That's OK,' Cassie said, pleasantly surprised. 'Goodnight, Erin.'

'G'night, Cassie. Sweet dreams,' Erin said sleepily.

Cassie snuggled down with Storm's little warm body next to her. The air was soon filled with soft snores, but she lay awake, enjoying looking out of the open-fronted shelter. The sky was deep purple and blazing with silver stars, like a million tiny diamonds. She wondered whether Storm could see the same stars in his own world.

Cassie felt a deep glow of happiness. 'I love having you here. I hope that you can stay with me forever,' she whispered to him.

Storm twisted his head to look at her, his midnight-blue eyes glowing brightly in the moonlight. 'That is not possible.

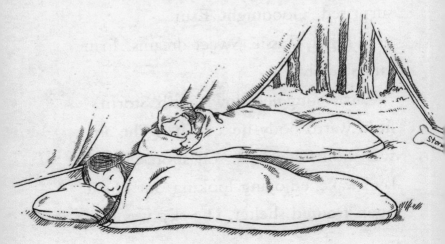

One day I must go back to my home world to face Shadow and lead the Moon-claw pack. Do you understand that, Cassie?' he woofed, his little square white face serious.

Cassie nodded sadly but she didn't want to think about that now. This moment was just perfect as it was. She kissed the top of Storm's fluffy white head. 'Sweet dreams,' she yawned as she drifted into sleep.

Chapter
SEVEN

It was cold and misty when Cassie
woke the following morning. No one
else was awake. She lay snuggled up
inside her sleeping bag for a while
longer, cuddling Storm's warm stocky
little body.

'This is nice and cosy, isn't it?' she
whispered, stroking his fluffy fur.

Storm looked up at her and she saw

his midnight-blue eyes darken with sadness. 'Yes. It is like being curled up in a safe den with . . . with . . .' he woofed and then tailed off into a deep sigh.

He's thinking of his mother and the Moon-claw pack in his own world, Cassie realized with a pang.

There must be something she could

do to help him feel better. 'I know!
How about an early morning walk?'
she suggested.

Storm pricked his ears, and his face
brightened a little. 'I would like that!'
He sprang out of the sleeping bag and
wagged his stumpy white tail.

The others were starting to wake up
now. So Cassie quickly dressed and
pulled on her boots. 'I'll fetch some
water for washing,' she called, picking
up a bucket.

As she and Storm went off in the
direction of the nearby stream, hazy
bars of sunlight pushed through the
mist hanging over the trees. There was a
smoky smell of frosty autumn leaves in
the air.

Storm tore around as usual, scrabbling

under fallen logs and sniffing at clumps of grass. He ran towards Cassie with a broken branch in his mouth and dropped it at her feet. Crouching down on to his front paws, he barked hopefully.

Cassie laughed and threw the branch for him to fetch. With a happy bark, Storm ran after it. He seemed to be feeling much happier than when he woke up – just as Cassie hoped he would.

She swung her arms as she walked, feeling perfectly happy. At the stream, she kneeled down to fill the bucket from a spring gushing down over some rocks. Storm was splashing about in the shallows a few metres away.

He jumped out on to the bank and came lolloping up to Cassie. His white fur stuck up in little wet peaks and there was a cheeky expression on his dripping face.

'Don't you dare —' Cassie began, but it was too late.

Storm's whole body shivered from head to foot as he shook himself. A shower of droplets splashed all over Cassie.

'Storm! You little terror! You did that on purpose!' she scolded laughingly. 'It's a good thing I'm wearing waterproofs.'

Storm beamed and stood up on his short back legs to paw at her trousers. His sharp puppy teeth were very white against his little black lips.

As they made their way back to camp, the delicious smell of frying bacon floated towards them.

'I like human food,' Storm yapped hungrily.

Cassie's mouth watered too. Why did food always smell so much better outdoors?

'Hello, love. You're an early bird this morning,' Mrs Yorke said as she turned rashers in the pan.

Mr Yorke was just opening a tin of tomatoes.

'Hiya, parents,' Cassie sang out as she put down the bucket of water. Storm's cheerfulness was infectious. 'I was wide awake, so I thought I'd do something useful.'

Her dad goggled his eyes. 'Quick, someone, call the police! Someone's stolen our Cassie and swapped her for this helpful, strangely cheerful girl!' he joked.

'Da-ad!' Cassie pretended to swipe him on the head.

She wished she could tell them that the reason why she was so happy was sitting there invisibly, wagging his little white tail. Cassie would have loved to see the look on their faces, but she

knew that she would never give away
Storm's secret.

That afternoon there were team games.
The most fun was when each person
took it in turn to be blindfolded and
then their team-mates talked them
through an obstacle course.

'I will make myself glow very
brightly and you will be able to see me
through the band round your eyes. You
can just follow me,' Storm woofed,
eager to take part.

'No. That would be cheating. I have
to do this myself, but thanks anyway,'
Cassie told him.

So instead, Storm joined in by
padding around on tiptoe behind the
person wearing the blindfold. Cassie

laughed so much that others began to
laugh too and even Erin joined in.

'I didn't think this game was *that*
funny!' Erin said, giggling and wiping
her eyes.

'It's not!' Cassie spluttered.

Later there was more firewood to
collect and then a short talk about
identifying and collecting wild
food. Time passed quickly for Cassie
and soon, after supper, everyone sat
round in a circle to do a task
together.

'You can make everything you need
from the materials around you. We're
going to make some cord from a plant
you can find growing almost anywhere,'
the instructor said, producing a bundle
of green stems.

'Ouch! Stinging nettles!' Cassie said nervously.

Storm twitched one ear. After having rushed about all day, he was lying next to her with his nose resting on his paws.

'Hold your nettle like this,' said the instructor, holding the stalks at an angle. 'Now, push firmly upwards to strip off the leaves. Try it. You won't get stung if you do it like this.'

'It would be far easier if we all wore gloves,' Mr Yorke joked.

Cassie grinned at him.

'Gloves?' Mr Ronson scoffed, obviously taking her dad seriously. 'I suppose you'll want a cushion to sit on next! Come on, man. Rise to the challenge!' He pushed up his sweatshirt sleeves, flexed his bulging muscles and then began rubbing his palms together noisily.

As her dad's face reddened, Cassie tingled with embarrassment on his behalf.

She couldn't stand the way Erin's dad always had to show off.

'Me first!' she shouted on impulse. Gritting her teeth she leaned forward and grabbed a big hairy nettle, exactly as the instructor had shown her. It didn't sting at all. She ran her hands upwards towards the top and the leaves fell off on to the grass.

'Da-dah!' Cassie crowed, waving the stripped stem in the air.

Mr Ronson looked at her in surprise. 'Not bad,' he said.

Coming from him, that was praise indeed,
Cassie thought.

As everyone got to work stripping
nettles, the instructor showed Cassie the
next stages in making cord.

Cassie felt a tiny tingle down her
spine. Next to her, little gold sparks

were starting to glisten in Storm's white fur.

She suddenly found herself smoothing, flattening, rolling and twisting, her nimble fingers flying. In half a minute she had her first ever piece of strong green cord. 'Storm. I can do this by myself,' she scolded gently.

Storm nodded. The sparks in his fur went out. He gave a contented sigh and began dozing as Cassie carried on making nettle cord by herself.

'Are you sure you haven't done this before? You're a natural,' the instructor said as the pile of cord in front of her grew.

'I've always loved making things. I guess it's some consolation for being rubbish at sports and stuff,' Cassie said modestly.

The instructor smiled. 'A good team needs "doers" and "makers". It's all about sharing skills.'

Cassie hadn't thought of it like that before. She felt a stir of pride. Perhaps being part of a team was something she could be good at after all.

On the other side of the circle, Erin grinned encouragingly.

Chapter
EIGHT

Later that evening, the instructors left for the cabin, intending to return early the following morning.

'You should all be fine by yourselves for a few hours. But we're not far away and we'll leave you a mobile phone in case of emergencies,' one of them said.

'I'll hold on to that phone,' Mr

Ronson said promptly, tucking it into his pocket.

It was another clear night. Trees cast long shadows in the moonlight as the Blues, Greens and Reds prepared for bed.

Cassie settled down with Storm. 'It's Sunday tomorrow. We go home after lunch. You're going to love it there,' she told him.

Storm gave a tiny woof and yawned sleepily. He turned round and round in

circles before settling comfortably with his head resting beneath Cassie's chin.

Cassie said her goodnights to everyone and instantly fell asleep.

She woke suddenly a few hours later, in the dark-grey light of dawn. There was a loud drumming noise all around her. At first Cassie couldn't understand what the noise was and then a cold raindrop splashed on to her nose.

She crawled to the open front of the shelter and peered out. Rain was coming down in torrents through the trees. In the semi-darkness, she could just see wriggly lines of water trickling past the shelter. A huge puddle glistened across what had been grass the night before and reached almost to the Greens' tent.

Storm stood up and shook himself. Lifting his nose, he sniffed the air. 'There is too much water. We could be in danger,' he yapped, flattening his ears.

'You mean floods? I'd better wake everyone up!' Cassie leapt up and scrambled into her clothes. She leaned over to shake Erin, who was nearest, and then woke both sets of parents. 'Quick! There's water everywhere!' she told them.

'It's just a bit of rain, for goodness' sake.' Mr Ronson's voice was muffled from deep within his sleeping bag. 'Stop fussing and go back to sleep.'

Storm lifted his lip in a soft growl and danced sideways, barking in annoyance. Cassie felt like doing the same thing.

'No! We have to move. Storm says so!' she burst out, hardly realizing what she'd said. Luckily, no one seemed to have heard her properly.

'What's that about a storm, Cass?' her dad asked sleepily, opening one eye. His hair was all sticking up. 'Are you sure you didn't just have a bad dream?'

'I'm not imagining this. Please, Dad, just take a look outside,' Cassie said desperately.

'OK. Anything for a bit of peace,' Mr Yorke groaned.

Suddenly, Erin cried out. 'There's water coming in. Ugh! My sleeping bag's getting soaked!'

Mr Yorke sat bolt upright. 'Crikey! Cassie's right. If we don't move soon, we'll be sitting in the middle of a lake!

Look, the Greens and Blues are already getting up!'

After that, there was a mad scramble to get dressed into waterproofs and roll up the sleeping bags. Cassie picked Storm up and cradled him in her arms, keeping him dry beneath her baggy anorak.

As they all splashed across to join up with the other families, the instructors' mobile phone rang. Mr Ronson answered it.

Cassie and Erin were closest to him and both heard some of what he said. 'No, there's no need for you to do that. It's not that bad here. Yes, I'm absolutely certain. We can make it back by ourselves,' Mr Ronson said confidently. 'OK. I'll explain to the others. No probs. Leave it to me.'

Cassie frowned in puzzlement. Something didn't seem quite right about the conversation. 'I wonder what's going on. What isn't there any need for the instructors to do?' she whispered to Storm.

Mr Ronson began speaking. 'We've been told to make our way back to the cabin. There's a short cut across a bridge, just over that ridge. I went and checked it out yesterday afternoon,' he explained.

'That seems a roundabout way to go, when we could go via the track we came in on,' Mr Yorke commented.

Mr Ronson shrugged. 'That's as may be. But this is the *Wild Wood Experiences* way and the sooner we get moving, the sooner we'll be back. Hurry up now; this way, everyone,' he said, waving one arm in a big arc.

'He'll be shouting "Wagons roll!" in a minute, like in those awful old cowboy films!' Cassie grumbled.

Her dad laughed. 'Remind me to buy him a sheriff's badge sometime.'

Cassie tramped along, feeling happy that they were all safe, despite the rain dripping from her anorak hood. Storm's little body was warm against her chest and she could smell his faint clean puppy scent. 'Are you OK in there?' she whispered, looking down at him.

Storm reached up and licked her chin. 'I am fine.'

The rain slowed and then stopped as they trudged along. After about ten minutes, they reached the top of the ridge. The ground sloped steeply downwards on the other side. At the bottom, Cassie could see the ditch with the wooden footbridge over it.

Suddenly, she heard fierce growling and barking through the trees. Cassie felt Storm stiffen and begin to tremble all over. 'What's wrong?' she asked softly.

'I think Shadow is close. He will have used his magic to make any dogs that are nearby into my enemies. Now he has set them on to me,' Storm whimpered softly, rolling his eyes in terror.

'Those dogs do sound like they're getting closer,' Cassie said worriedly. 'How will I be able to tell if they're coming for you?'

Storm whimpered and Cassie could feel his heart beating wildly. 'They will have fierce pale eyes and extra-long teeth.'

The sound of growling was even louder. Cassie felt a leap of fear. Storm was in terrible danger! She racked her brains as she tried to think of some way of protecting the tiny puppy.

A memory stirred within her. In one of her favourite books, Jilly Atkins had been tracked by a hungry bear and had escaped by rubbing something very

nasty indeed all over herself to disguise
her scent.

'That's it!' Cassie burst out. Without a
second thought, she pretended to lose
her balance and slip over. 'Oh,' she cried
as she skidded for real and both legs
shot from beneath her.

She landed on her backside with a
teeth-rattling jolt. Gathering speed,
Cassie went sliding downwards in a
slippery muddy avalanche of half-rotten
leaves.

Chapter
NINE

Taking care to cradle Storm in both hands, Cassie twisted sideways and began rolling over and over down the slope. She wanted to make certain that she was covered in smelly stuff from head to foot.

As Cassie tumbled to the bottom, she found herself heading towards a big clump of brambles, but couldn't put out her hands to stop herself. Sharp thorns tore at her clothes and made deep scratches in her skin, but Cassie hardly noticed them.

Tearing herself free, she scrambled to her feet. A strong earthy pong rose up around her.

'Perfect! No enemy dogs will be able

to smell you through this stuff,' Cassie said.

'Thank you, Cassie,' Storm whined softly. 'That was very brave. You could have been badly hurt.'

'I couldn't bear anything to happen to you,' Cassie said. 'Oh,' she gasped, as the scratches started throbbing now that the excitement was over.

'You *are* hurt! I will make you better,' Storm yapped.

Cassie felt a familiar prickling down her spine as Storm huffed out a glittery puppy breath. The softly gleaming cloud floated into the air and then sprinkled down on to Cassie like Christmas glitter. As the golden dust dissolved into her muddy clothes, she felt the soreness fading and all the rips and tears mended themselves instantly.

'Thanks, Storm,' she said, stroking his little warm ears. 'I think you'd better stay inside my anorak until we're completely certain that those fierce dogs have gone.'

The fear was starting to fade from Storm's deep blue eyes, but he nodded. 'I think so too.'

'Cassie!' her mum shouted in a panicky voice, hurtling down the slope ahead of the others. 'Are you hurt?'

'No. I'm just a bit shaken up,' Cassie replied.

'Thank goodness for that. I can't believe you've escaped without even a scratch or the tiniest rip in your clothes. You're a very lucky girl!'

'I know,' Cassie said. *I'm the luckiest*

girl in the whole world — I've got Storm for a friend, she thought.

Cassie's mum wrinkled her nose. 'But just look at the state of you! Phew! You smell dreadful!'

'I don't mind,' Cassie said happily.

'You're going to need a shower when we get back to the cabin,' her dad said on reaching her. 'You clumsy old sausage. Fancy falling down that

slope. It's the sort of thing I usually do!' he said.

Cassie realized that he was about to give her a comforting hug, despite the smelly mud. 'No, don't, Dad! You'll get all stinky too,' she said quickly, backing away. If he squeezed her, he'd be sure to feel Storm's sturdy little body beneath her anorak.

Mr Ronson came stamping over. 'For goodness' sake! Can't that girl do anything right? Of all the useless –'

'Don't, Dad! Cassie's OK,' Erin cried from just behind him. 'And it's not her fault anyway. We didn't have to come this way, did we?'

Cassie's jaw dropped in astonishment. Did Erin just stick up for her?

'What does Erin mean?' asked Mr Yorke.

Mr Ronson looked rather uncomfortable as the others gazed at him enquiringly.

A light seemed to go on in Cassie's head as she remembered the mobile-phone conversation. It was starting to make sense now. 'You weren't told to bring us back this way, were you? That was all your own idea!'

'Is this true, Ronson?' asked one of the other dads.

Mr Ronson nodded slowly. 'They were going to send a van to pick us up and told us to meet it at the track. But I told them not to bother. We came here for the challenge, didn't we? I thought you'd all welcome the chance of getting back under our own steam.'

'But you didn't bother to ask us if we

agreed with you, did you?' Mr Yorke
said angrily. 'As a team member, you're
the worst. Not to mention that Cassie
could have been badly hurt when she
tumbled down that muddy slope!'

'But I'm fine, Dad!' Cassie protested.

'That's not the point.' Her dad
squared his shoulders and stood his
ground in front of the taller man. 'What
do you say, Ronson?'

Mr Ronson shifted his feet. 'OK. I

admit that I was wrong. I'm sorry, everyone.' He turned to Cassie. 'And I'm truly sorry that you almost got hurt. I'll call the cabin right now and tell them to send the van for us after all.'

'You do that!' Mr Yorke said. He looked at Cassie and her mum. 'Let's skirt round this ridge and make our way to the track.'

Everyone else began following as the Yorkes set off. Cassie hung back to thank Erin, but the older girl avoided her eyes and linked arms with her dad.

Cassie sighed as she went to catch up with her mum and dad. 'I thought Erin might feel like walking back together, but she doesn't seem to want anything to do with me,' she whispered disappointedly to Storm.

'Perhaps she just needs more time,' Storm woofed wisely. 'It could not have been easy for her to stand up to her father.'

Cassie nodded. 'That's true.' She hoped that Storm was right about Erin needing more time, but she was starting to think that they would never be friends.

Chapter
TEN

To Cassie's immense relief, there was no more growling or barking as she and Storm made their way to the track, along with the others.

'I think this smelly mud has done the trick. Shadow's dogs must have gone past,' Cassie said.

Storm nodded, his midnight-blue eyes thoughtful. 'Your plan has worked for the moment. But I sense that those dogs are not too far away. If they return, I may have to leave suddenly.'

Cassie felt a pang as she realized that she didn't feel ready ever to let her magical little friend go. She loved being with Storm so much.

'I'm looking forward to getting

warm,' she said, deliberately changing the subject. 'And I want a mega-sized mug of hot chocolate and a mountain of biscuits, so I can share them with you!'

Storm perked up and licked his little chops. 'That sounds good!'

A big minibus was waiting on the track. The group all piled inside. Cassie lifted the bottom of her anorak, so that Storm could crawl out. She sat with him on her lap, stroking his fluffy white fur.

Back at the cabin, everyone began changing into dry clothes. With so many people inside, it was rather cramped. There were wet boots, rucksacks and waterproofs everywhere.

'Come on, young lady. Let's get you

straight into the shower,' said Cassie's mum. 'Here you are. You can change into these.' She thrust a bundle of dry clothes into her arms.

Cassie went into the large washroom. She soaped and scrubbed herself, enjoying the hot water. Steam filled the shower cubicle, so that Cassie didn't notice Storm press himself into the corner by the door and then keep looking round nervously.

After Cassie finished drying herself, she pulled on her jeans and T-shirt and dry trainers.

Just as Cassie and Storm came out of the shower, Cassie almost bumped into Erin, who was bent over with her head under a wall-mounted dryer.

'Hi,' Cassie said.

Erin stood up and flicked her damp hair back. 'Hi.'

Cassie chewed her lip, trying to think of something to say. 'I'm . . . er . . .' she began.

'No, let me go first,' Erin said. She took a deep breath and then out it all came in a rush. 'I don't suppose you'd . . . er . . . want to come to my house sometime, would you? I know I've been a brat and my dad can be a bit stern and bossy, but he's OK when you get to know him better. And I've just got this brilliant new computer game with Jilly Atkins in and I thought we could – what?' she asked, as Cassie stood there open-mouthed.

'I can't believe it. You like Jilly Atkins?' Cassie said delightedly.

Erin nodded. 'I absolutely love her. I've read all her books, except the new one.'

'Me too! I'm reading the new one now. You can borrow it after me, if you like,' Cassie said, smiling all over her face.

Erin beamed back at her. 'Cool! So you'll get your dad to bring you over?'

'I'd love to!' Cassie said.

This weekend had turned out really well after all. Cassie had to admit that the team building had worked a treat — at least for her and Erin.

She was still taking these amazing developments in, when Storm suddenly gave a sharp whine of terror and shot towards the washroom door. At that moment, someone came in and Storm bolted straight out of the gap.

Cassie's tummy clenched. Storm's enemies must have come back. He was in terrible danger. Leaping forward, she ran after Storm. 'Back in a minute,' she called to a puzzled-looking Erin.

Cassie pounded down the corridor. Right at the end of it, she saw Storm's stocky little white form dash round a door with *Storeroom* written on it. From somewhere just outside, she could hear loud snarls and growls.

As Cassie reached the storeroom, a dazzling flash of bright gold light streamed out of it. Nervous about what might happen, she slowly opened the door more widely and went inside.

There was Storm, a tiny helpless puppy no longer, but his true majestic self: a beautiful young silver-grey wolf with glowing midnight-blue eyes. An older wolf with a gentle face, whom Cassie guessed was his mother, stood next to him.

And then Cassie knew that Storm was leaving for good. She was going to have to be very brave. She rushed over and Storm allowed her to hug him one last time.

'I'll never forget you, Storm,' Cassie said, her voice breaking as she buried her face in his thick soft fur.

'You have been a good friend. I will remember you too,' Storm said in a deep velvety growl.

Cassie took a step back just as an ugly growl sounded right outside the

door. 'Go. Save yourself, Storm!' she urged, her heart aching.

There was a final burst of brilliant gold light and a bright shower of sparks floated down all around Cassie and crackled on the storeroom floor. Storm and his mother faded and then were gone. The growl was abruptly cut off and silence fell.

Cassie felt her throat sting with tears. She was going to miss Storm terribly, but at least she knew he was safe. And she would always have her secret memories of the wonderful adventure they'd shared.

'Cassie? Where are you?' called Erin's voice from the corridor.

'Coming!' Cassie called, making for the door. She took a deep breath and

silently wished magic puppy Storm and
his Moon-claw pack well as, smiling,
she went to find her new friend for
some adventures of their own.

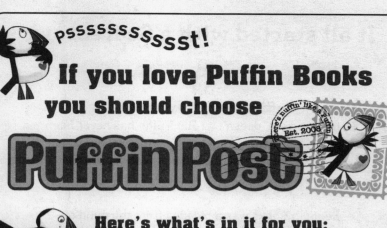

Psssssssssssst!

If you love Puffin Books you should choose

Puffin Post

Here's what's in it for you:

⭐ 6 magazines

⭐ 6 free books a year (of your choice)

⭐ The chance to see YOUR writing in print

PLUS

⭐ Exclusive author features

⭐ Articles

⭐ Quizzes

⭐ Competitions and games

And that's not all.
You get PRESENTS too.

Simply subscribe here to become a member
puffinpost.co.uk
and wait for your copy to decorate your doorstep.

(WARNING – reading *Puffin Post* may make you late for school.)

It all started with a Scarecrow.

Puffin is seventy years old.
Sounds ancient, doesn't it? But Puffin has never been
so lively. We're always on the lookout for the next big
idea, which is how it began all those years ago.

Penguin Books was a big idea from the mind of
a man called Allen Lane, who in 1935 invented
the quality paperback and changed the world.
**And from great Penguins, great Puffins grew,
changing the face of children's books forever.**

The first four Puffin Picture Books were hatched in 1940 and the
first Puffin story book featured a man with broomstick arms called
Worzel Gummidge. In 1967 Kaye Webb, Puffin Editor, started the
Puffin Club, promising to **'make children into readers'**.
She kept that promise and over 200,000 children became
devoted Puffineers through their quarterly instalments of
Puffin Post, which is now back for a new generation.

Many years from now, we hope you'll look back and
remember Puffin with a smile. **No matter what your age
or what you're into, there's a Puffin for everyone.**
The possibilities are endless, but one thing is for sure:
whether it's a picture book or a paperback, a sticker book
or a hardback, **if it's got that little Puffin
on it – it's bound to be good.**